Captive Devotion

The Millionaire's Pretty Woman Series, Volume 2

Lexy Timms

Published by Dark Shadow Publishing, 2021.

This is a work of fiction. Similarities to real people, places, or events are entirely coincidental.

CAPTIVE DEVOTION

First edition. July 30, 2021.

Copyright © 2021 Lexy Timms.

Written by Lexy Timms.

Also by Lexy Timms

A Bad Boy Bullied Romance
I Hate You
I Hate You A Little Bit
I Hate You A Little Bit More

A Bump in the Road Series
Expecting Love
Selfless Act
Doctor's Orders

A Burning Love Series
Spark of Passion
Flame of Desire
Blaze of Ecstasy

A Chance at Forever Series
Forever Perfect
Forever Desired

Forever Together

A Dark Mafia Romance Series
Taken By The Mob Boss
Truce With The Mob Boss
Taking Over the Mob Boss
Trouble For The Mob Boss
Tailored By The Mob Boss
Tricking the Mob Boss

A Dating App Series
I've Been Matched
You've Been Matched
We've Been Matched

A "Kind of" Billionaire
Taking a Risk
Safety in Numbers
Pretend You're Mine

A Maybe Series
Maybe I Should
Maybe I Shouldn't
Maybe I Did

Assisting the Boss Series
Billion Reasons
Duke of Delegation
Late Night Meetings
Delegating Love
Suitors and Admirers

BBW Romance Series
Capturing Her Beauty
Pursuing Her Dreams
Tracing Her Curves

Beating the Biker Series
Making Her His
Making the Break
Making of Them

Betrayal at the Bay Series
Devil's Bay
Devil's Deceit
Devil's Duplicity

Billionaire Banker Series
Banking on Him

Price of Passion
Investing in Love
Knowing Your Worth
Treasured Forever
Banking on Christmas
Billionaire Banker Box Set Books #1-3

Billionaire CEO Brothers
Tempting the Player
Late Night Boardroom
Reviewing the Perfomance
Result of Passion
Directing the Next Move
Touching the Assets

Billionaire Hitman Series
The Hit
The Job
The Run

Billionaire Holiday Romance Series
Driving Home for Christmas
The Valentine Getaway
Cruising Love
Billionaire Holiday Romance Box Set

Billionaire in Disguise Series
Facade
Illusion
Charade

Billionaire Secrets Series
The Secret
Freedom
Courage
Trust
Impulse
Billionaire Secrets Box Set Books #1-3

Blind Sight Series
See Me
Fix Me
Eyes On Me

Branded Series
Money or Nothing
What People Say
Give and Take

Building Billions

Building Billions - Part 1
Building Billions - Part 2
Building Billions - Part 3

Butler & Heiress Series
To Serve
For Duty
No Chore
All Wrapped Up

Change of Heart Series
The Heart Needs
The Heart Wants
The Heart Knows

Counting the Billions
Counting the Days
Counting On You
Counting the Kisses

Cry Wolf Reverse Harem Series
Beautiful & Wild
Misunderstood
Never Tamed

Darkest Night Series
Savage
Vicious
Brutal
Sinful
Fierce

Diamond in the Rough Anthology
Billionaire Rock
Billionaire Rock - part 2

Dirty Little Taboo Series
Flirting Touch
Denying Pleasure
Forbidding Desire
Craving Passion

Dominating PA Series
Her Personal Assistant - Part 1
Her Personal Assistant - Part 2
Her Personal Assistant Box Set

Fake Billionaire Series
Faking It

Temporary CEO
Caught in the Act
Never Tell A Lie
Fake Christmas
Fake Billionaire Box Set #1-3

Firehouse Romance Series
Caught in Flames
Burning With Desire
Craving the Heat
Firehouse Romance Complete Collection

Forging Billions Series
Dirty Money
Petty Cash
Payment Required

For His Pleasure
Elizabeth
Georgia
Madison

Fortune Riders MC Series
Billionaire Biker
Billionaire Ransom
Billionaire Misery

Fortune Riders Box Set - Books #1-3

Fragile Series
Fragile Touch
Fragile Kiss
Fragile Love

Great Temptation Series
The Devil's Footsteps
Heaven's Command
Mortals Surrender

Hades' Spawn Motorcycle Club
One You Can't Forget
One That Got Away
One That Came Back
One You Never Leave
One Christmas Night
Hades' Spawn MC Complete Series

Hard Rocked Series
Rhyme
Harmony
Lyrics

Heart of Stone Series
The Protector
The Guardian
The Warrior

Heart of the Battle Series
Celtic Viking
Celtic Rune
Celtic Mann
Heart of the Battle Series Box Set

Heistdom Series
Master Thief
Goldmine
Diamond Heist
Smile For Me
Your Move
Green With Envy
Saving Money

Highlander Wolf Series
Pack Run
Pack Land
Pack Rules

Hollyweird Fae Series
Inception of Gold
Disruption of Magic
Guardians of Twilight

How To Love A Spy
The Secret
The Secret Life
The Secret Wife

Just About Series
About Love
About Truth
About Forever
Just About Box Set Books #1-3

Justice Series
Seeking Justice
Finding Justice
Chasing Justice
Pursuing Justice
Justice - Complete Series

Karma Series

Walk Away
Make Him Pay
Perfect Revenge

Kissed by Billions
Kissed by Passion
Kissed by Desire
Kissed by Love

Leaning Towards Trouble
Trouble
Discord
Tenacity

Love on the Sea Series
Ships Ahoy
Rough Sea
High Tide

Love You Series
Love Life
Need Love
My Love

Managing the Billionaire

Never Enough
Worth the Cost
Secret Admirers
Chasing Affection
Pressing Romance
Timeless Memories
Managing the Billionaire Box Set Books #1-3

Managing the Bosses Series
The Boss
The Boss Too
Who's the Boss Now
Love the Boss
I Do the Boss
Wife to the Boss
Employed by the Boss
Brother to the Boss
Senior Advisor to the Boss
Forever the Boss
Christmas With the Boss
Billionaire in Control
Billionaire Makes Millions
Billionaire at Work
Precious Little Thing
Priceless Love
Valentine Love
The Cost of Freedom
Trick or Treat
The Night Before Christmas
Gift for the Boss - Novella 3.5
Managing the Bosses Box Set #1-3

Managing the Bosses Novellas

Mislead by the Bad Boy Series
Deceived
Provoked
Betrayed

Model Mayhem Series
Shameless
Modesty
Imperfection

Moment in Time
Highlander's Bride
Victorian Bride
Modern Day Bride
A Royal Bride
Forever the Bride

Mountain Millionaire Series
Close to the Ridge
Crossing the Bluff
Climbing the Mount

My Best Friend's Sister

Hometown Calling
A Perfect Moment
Thrown in Together

My Darker Side Series
Darkest Hour
Time to Stop
Against the Light

Neverending Dream Series
Neverending Dream - Part 1
Neverending Dream - Part 2
Neverending Dream - Part 3
Neverending Dream - Part 4
Neverending Dream - Part 5
Neverending Dream Box Set Books #1-3

Outside the Octagon
Submit
Fight
Knockout

Protecting Diana Series
Her Bodyguard
Her Defender
Her Champion

Her Protector
Her Forever
Protecting Diana Box Set Books #1-3

Protecting Layla Series
His Mission
His Objective
His Devotion

Racing Hearts Series
Rush
Pace
Fast

Regency Romance Series
The Duchess Scandal - Part 1
The Duchess Scandal - Part 2

Reverse Harem Series
Primals
Archaic
Unitary

R&S Rich and Single Series
Alex Reid

Parker
Sebastian

Saving Forever
Saving Forever - Part 1
Saving Forever - Part 2
Saving Forever - Part 3
Saving Forever - Part 4
Saving Forever - Part 5
Saving Forever - Part 6
Saving Forever Part 7
Saving Forever - Part 8
Saving Forever Boxset Books #1-3

Secrets & Lies Series
Strange Secrets
Evading Secrets
Inspiring Secrets
Lies and Secrets
Mastering Secrets
Alluring Secrets
Secrets & Lies Box Set Books #1-3

Shifting Desires Series
Jungle Heat
Jungle Fever
Jungle Blaze

Sin Series
Payment for Sin
Atonement Within
Declaration of Love

Southern Romance Series
Little Love Affair
Siege of the Heart
Freedom Forever
Soldier's Fortune

Spanked Series
Passion
Playmate
Pleasure

Spelling Love Series
The Author
The Book Boyfriend
The Words of Love

Strength & Style
Suits You, Sir
Tailor Made

Taboo Wedding Series
He Loves Me Not
With This Ring
Happily Ever After

Tattooist Series
Confession of a Tattooist
Surrender of a Tattooist
Heart of a Tattooist
Hopes & Dreams of a Tattooist

Tennessee Romance
Whisky Lullaby
Whisky Melody
Whisky Harmony

The Bad Boy Alpha Club
Battle Lines - Part 1
Battle Lines

The Brush Of Love Series
Every Night
Every Day
Every Time

Every Way
Every Touch
The Brush of Love Series Box Set Books #1-3

The City of Mayhem Series
True Mayhem
Relentless Chaos

The Debt
The Debt: Part 1 - Damn Horse
The Debt: Complete Collection

The Fire Inside Series
Dare Me
Defy Me
Burn Me

The Gentleman's Club Series
Gambler
Player
Wager

The Golden Mail
Hot Off the Press
Extra! Extra!

Read All About It
Stop the Press
Breaking News
This Just In
The Golden Mail Box Set Books #1-3

The Lucky Billionaire Series
Lucky Break
Streak of Luck
Lucky in Love

The Millionaire's Pretty Woman Series
Perfect Stranger
Captive Devotion
Sweet Temptations

The Sound of Breaking Hearts Series
Disruption
Destroy
Devoted

The University of Gatica Series
The Recruiting Trip
Faster
Higher
Stronger

Dominate
No Rush
University of Gatica - The Complete Series

T.N.T. Series
Troubled Nate Thomas - Part 1
Troubled Nate Thomas - Part 2
Troubled Nate Thomas - Part 3

Toxic Touch Series
Noxious
Lethal
Willful
Tainted
Craved
Toxic Touch Box Set Books #1-3

Undercover Boss Series
Marketing
Finance
Legal

Undercover Series
Perfect For Me
Perfect For You
Perfect For Us

Unknown Identity Series
Unknown
Unpublished
Unexposed
Unsure
Unwritten
Unknown Identity Box Set: Books #1-3

Unlucky Series
Unlucky in Love
UnWanted
UnLoved Forever

War Torn Letters Series
My Sweetheart
My Darling
My Beloved

Wet & Wild Series
Stormy Love
Savage Love
Secure Love

Worth It Series

Worth Billions
Worth Every Cent
Worth More Than Money

You & Me - A Bad Boy Romance
Just Me
Touch Me
Kiss Me

Standalone
Wash
Loving Charity
Summer Lovin'
Love & College
Billionaire Heart
First Love
Frisky and Fun Romance Box Collection
Beating Hades' Bikers
Everyone Loves a Bad Boy

Watch for more at www.lexytimms.com.

Copyright 2021 By LEXY TIMMS

ALL RIGHTS RESERVED. No part of this publication may be reproduced, stored in or introduced into a retrieval system, or transmitted, in any form, or by any means (electronic, mechanical, photocopying, recording, or otherwise) without the prior written permission of both the copyright owner and the above publisher of this book.

This is a work of fiction. Names, characters, places, brands, media, and incidents are either the product of the author's imagination or are used fictitiously. Any resemblance to an actual person, living or dead, events, or locales is entirely coincidental. The author acknowledges the trademarked status and trademark owners of various products referenced in this work of fiction, which have been used without permission. The publication/use of these trademarks is not authorized, associated with, or sponsored by the trademark owners.

. . ⚓ . .

All rights reserved.
Captive Devotion
The Millionaire's Pretty Woman Series Book 2
Copyright 2021 by Lexy Timms
Cover by: Book Cover by Design[1]

---

1. http://bookcoverbydesign.co.uk/

The Millionaire's Pretty Woman Series

Book 1 – Perfect Stranger
Book 2 – Captive Devotion
Book 3 – Sweet Temptations

Find Lexy Timms:

LEXY TIMMS NEWSLETTER:
http://eepurl.com/9i0vD
Lexy Timms Facebook Page:
https://www.facebook.com/SavingForever
Lexy Timms Website:
http://www.lexytimms.com

Want to read more...
For **FREE?**
Sign up for Lexy Timms' newsletter
And she'll send you updates on new releases, ARC copies of books and a whole lotta fun!
Sign up for news and updates!
http://eepurl.com/9i0vD

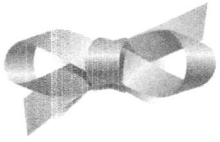

Captive Devotion Blurb

IN THAT PERFECT STRANGER, I found my fairytale...

Olivia Cadwell is finding herself in an impossible situation. She knows she has to leave Leo Folley and his privileged life if she's going to protect him from the people who are after her. She knows she can't work in his office anymore, if she wants to protect him from his own board of investors.

Unfortunately, she's also fallen in love with him. And that's going to make leaving a whole lot harder.

When she runs into her own father outside of Leo's office, though, things get a whole lot more complicated. And the stakes get a whole lot higher.

A job is a job... until you're the bosses pretty woman.

CHAPTER 1

OLIVIA

I snapped my mouth shut, horrified that I'd said anything—and especially something as incriminating as what I'd said—and stared at Leo.

He didn't know that I'd been lying to him. He didn't know that I'd been hiding an entire past—and the abuse that had happened there, and an absent father, and a mother who insisted on dating guys that were the opposite of all right.

He did know that I hadn't graduated from college. But that was the extent of it.

So why in the ever-loving fuck had I thought I needed to come in, see him on the phone looking shocked, and blurt out that I could explain everything?

Say what you want about people keeping secrets, but in that moment, I realized that the actions of a guilty conscience are very real, very scary things. I'd been feeling guilty about keeping things from him from essentially the first moment he walked into my life, but I'd known that there were very good reasons for keeping my secrets. Unfortunately, my subconscious seemed to have other ideas.

Equally unfortunately, my subconscious had chosen that moment to grab hold of my physical actions and lead me right into exposing myself.

"What?" Leo asked quietly.

He glanced down at the phone still in his hand, frowning like he'd forgotten it was there, and then put it gently down. Then he looked up at me once more, his eyes full of questions.

And suspicion.

And dammit, it was the suspicion I saw in them that broke my heart cleanly into pieces.

Because that suspicion meant that he *did* know what I was talking about when I said I could explain. It meant that the phone call—which he'd taken so suddenly, and which had carried him right out of the kitchen and away from me, his voice hushed and his shoulders hunched over like he was trying to protect it even more—had been exactly what I'd been worried it was.

"Why are you looking into me, Leo?" I asked, following his question with my own.

"Don't change the subject, Olivia," he said evenly. "Or… wait, is Olivia even your name? Or should I be calling you something else?"

I felt like the floor had just fallen out from under me, leaving nothing but open air and danger underneath me. I'd been feeling so safe here. So secure, and so… well, not loved, necessarily, but at least accepted. I'd been having a good time.

No, I hadn't planned to stay much longer. In fact, I was already making plans for how I was going to leave—and whether I'd tell Leo before I went. But that hadn't changed the fact that I really, really liked this guy.

It certainly didn't change the fact that I wanted him to like me back.

"My name is Olivia," I told him firmly. "And don't *you* change the subject. Why are you looking into my past? What is it that you need to know so badly that you evidently hired someone else to find out about it for you?"

His eyes narrowed, but he didn't throw me off. Instead, he thought about it for a moment and then nodded, having come to some kind of decision.

"You know the board isn't happy with me hiring you in the first place. They're even less happy when I can't give them any background information."

I saw him start to add something else... and stop himself.

I saw him trying to decide whether he should add anything more. And honestly, I paused for several moments, waiting for him to do just that.

Because we'd been living together for a week now. Not together, but at least under the same roof. I'd been working in his office. More importantly, we'd stayed up half the night talking on several occasions and slept together more than once.

The man had touched me in ways no one else ever had, and I'd been under the impression that I'd had the same effect on him.

So why the cold, hard answer about his board and nothing else?

And did I actually care? Could I *afford* to?

Well, I decided a moment later, if he could be cold and hard, then I could, too.

"The board doesn't have a right to know what I've been through," I told him bluntly. "Though I suppose I owe it to you to give you the truth. You've certainly asked often enough. You're right. I'm not using my real name. I'm using someone else's, and there's a good fucking reason for that. I left my hometown because someone was after me, and I'm trying to keep that someone from coming after anyone else. But don't worry, Leo. I won't be your problem much longer. Pretty soon I'll be long gone, and then you won't have to worry about what your board thinks of you hiring a woman they don't know anything about. Pretty soon, I'll be nothing more than a memory."

I turned and made for my room before he could give me any answer to that admittedly very dramatic statement, and honestly, I didn't know if I'd have been able to listen even if he *had* answered. I was too busy going through all the possible repercussions of him having done this digging.

Yeah, I understood him wanting to know more about me. Shit, the man had basically told me his entire history and then introduced me to his family. He was an open fucking book. It had to be driving him crazy that I wasn't doing the same thing for him. He'd asked me time and again where I'd come from and why I'd left, and I'd pushed him off every single time.

For his own good, I remembered, reaching my suite and yanking the door open. I'd done it for his own good. Because there was a shadow in my past, one named Roger, and he was dangerous. Too much poking and he might come right out of the past and into the present, and that was the last thing I wanted. The last time I'd talked to Roger, he'd been threatening to come find me.

I wasn't stupid enough to think it was beyond him to do it. And I knew damn well that if he did, everyone around me would be collateral damage.

Which was exactly why I'd been keeping it secret. The less anyone else poked at my past, the less chance there was of Roger figuring out where I was and showing up at my front door.

At Leo's front door.

And now Leo had quite possibly ruined everything I'd done to keep him safe, just because of his damned curiosity.

I slammed the door behind me and stalked across the room, torn between wanting to start packing right now, just to get it done, and then calling a car to come pick me up in the morning… and wanting to run back out into the kitchen and into Leo's arms.

I wanted to stay with him, I realized. Yes, this had started out as a one-week engagement and a way to get some money so I could actually get a hotel. Yes, I'd only planned to stay through his big event. The event that he'd hired me to accompany him to.

Yes, I was already planning on leaving again just as soon as he got things sorted at his company and found a replacement for me in the accounting department.

None of that had changed, I realized, my heart cracking once more. I still didn't have a place here, and if anything, him digging into my past—and for all I knew, putting himself at even more risk for discovery—just confirmed that I had to get out of here sooner rather than later.

Just this afternoon, I'd been trying to figure out whether I could find a way—or a reason—to stay with this man who had somehow welcomed me into his life when he didn't know anything about me.

Now, as I collapsed on my bed and brought a pillow over my head to shut out the light, I was trying to figure out how quickly I needed to leave.

. . ❦ . .

I WOKE UP FEELING GROGGY and disgusting, like I'd gone to bed without bothering to wash off my makeup or brush my teeth.

Three seconds of blinking dazedly at the ceiling and I remembered that that was exactly what I'd done.

Three more seconds and I remembered everything else, too. The dinner we'd been working on. Or rather... the dinner Leo had been working on when I found him in the kitchen.

The dinner he'd interrupted to take a phone call from someone I now suspected was his own private PI.

The look on his face when I caught him on the phone. My immediate statement that I could explain. His own excuse of not knowing enough about me to satisfy the board.

The shattering realization that I really had to go, because staying here would just encourage more digging—and more ways for Roger to hear about that digging and discover Leo himself.

I groaned and turned over, every muscle in my body feeling like I'd been running sprints rather than sleeping, and stared out the window.

I had to admit, the view was glorious. Leo lived in the apartment on the top floor of the tallest building in Minneapolis—or at least I thought it probably was—as he had the view to prove it. I could see across the city, the parks dotting the buildings like bright green gems, the sky blue and gorgeous beyond the skyline.

And beyond that...

Beyond that, the freeway that wound toward the rest of Minnesota. More specifically, toward my hometown, where Roger awaited, probably still expecting me to turn up on his front door with apologies for having dared to go to my mother and tell her that she should leave him if he was hitting her.

I grimaced at the train of thought. The man was a real piece of work. I'd seen him hit my mother and said something, and then I'd told her that she needed to leave him if he was going to treat her like that.

She'd told him, and he'd called me with threats and promises about what he'd do if I ever talked that way about him again. So I'd done the only thing I *could* do: I'd packed up what I absolutely couldn't live without and run.

And here I was, still running.

I hated that I wasn't just standing up to him. Hated that I wasn't going home to fight for my mother—or waiting here for him to find me so we could have that fight on ground I knew better than he did.

The problem was, even having that fight here, where I'd be on more solid footing and had friends I thought I could count on, came with a big, big asterisk.

Leo.

The minute Roger knew I was in Minneapolis and came looking for me, he'd find out about Leo. And I knew I wasn't exaggerating when I thought that Roger would do pretty much anything he could to ruin the man who'd gone out of his way to help me.

He'd take me down, and he'd take Leo down just for standing in the way.

And I wasn't about to let that happen.

Then another thought occurred to me, and I sat up, trying to get better blood flow to my brain.

Because last night, I'd thought that leaving this morning—leaving as quickly as possible—was the answer. I'd thought that it would keep Leo safe. If I was no longer in the picture, Roger would have no reason to come to Minneapolis or find Leo or do anything to hurt him.

Leaving would protect Leo. Or at least I'd thought.

But now, lying here and considering the entire picture without the handicap of being freshly hurt by finding out that Leo had hired a PI to look into my past, I was seeing things a whole different way.

If I disappeared, Leo would search for me. And if he heard someone was after me—and let's face it, he might—he would try to protect me. It was just who he was.

A hero, even if he didn't want to be.

He'd end up putting himself in danger even if I disappeared on him, and he deserved better than that.

He deserved a real explanation. I didn't want to give it to him, and everything in me was screaming that it could lead straight into trouble, but when it came down to it, Leo had been very, very good to me over the past week. He'd offered me safety and warmth and as much hot water as I could use.

Could I really just leave him without giving him what he was asking for and at least making sure he was safe?

I couldn't. I knew I couldn't.

"Damned hero," I muttered to myself, throwing my legs over the edge of the bed and dragging myself up and toward the shower. "Always trying to save someone."

I hated that about myself, but it didn't change the fact that it was true.

I couldn't leave Leo here to fend for himself. I owed him an answer. And that meant I was going to work today, I guessed. Going to work and going straight into his office to give him the answers he'd been asking for since I'd met him.

CHAPTER 2

LEO

• • ❧ • •

I WAS STARING AT MY computer, getting a whole lot of nothing done thanks to my total inability to focus on work today rather than the girl I hoped was still in my apartment, in her room and sound asleep.

Olivia. If that was actually her name.

I thought it had to be, personally. She responded to it too easily for it to be something she'd just picked up a day before I met her. Of course, I guessed she could have been using it for some time so she got used to it, but it didn't feel right. She *felt* like an Olivia to me.

Though it was anyone's guess whether *that* actually meant anything.

At that moment, there was a knock on my door, and Jack opened it up without waiting for an answer. Just like he'd always done.

"Jack," I said wearily. "What's up? I don't have a lot of brainpower for anything complicated today."

"So I see," he replied, looking me up and down once. "You look like you didn't sleep last night."

He wasn't wrong. After Olivia had stormed out, I'd called Pete, the PI, back to see if he could give me anything, and after being told no, he couldn't, I'd gone to my room, leaving the kitchen a mess in my hurry to get someplace quiet and think. I'd just found out that no one with Olivia's name and age came from the town she'd called her hometown, and when she found out I was looking into her past, she'd flown off the handle and stormed to her own room without any explanation.

I had needed quiet very badly. And though I'd wanted to go talk to her about what had happened—get the real answer—I'd also known that I needed to give her some space before I tried that.

Unfortunately, the peace and quiet of my room hadn't given me much in the way of peace of mind. I'd sat on my bed all night, trying to get my brain to give me something good and failing, and when my alarm went off this morning, I'd chastised myself for having stayed in my room rather than doing anything useful and then dragged myself to the shower.

That could also be one of the reasons for my inability to work today, now that I thought about it. Lack of sleep had never been a good look for me.

"I *didn't* sleep last night," I told him bluntly. "What's up?"

He was just opening his mouth to tell me when my eyes slid past him...

And caught Olivia herself strolling past my office, her eyes darting from Jack to me and back again, her mouth pursed in thought and her face paler than I'd ever seen it before.

She had dark shadows under her eyes and equally dark shadows behind them and looked like she'd slept as badly as I had.

I was up and moving before Jack even started talking, brushing past him in my hurry to get to the girl I couldn't get off my mind. I caught her at the mouth of the hallway, right as it opened up onto the main floor, where all of the cubicles lived.

Which meant that when I grabbed her hand and brought her back around to face me, we were in clear view of nearly everyone on the fucking floor.

I didn't care. I'd been waiting to talk to her again since last night when she left me so suddenly, and I hadn't expected to see her again until I went home for dinner. Hell, I hadn't even been sure I'd see her then, either. I'd been afraid she would have run from the apartment already.

And if she had, I was positive she wouldn't have left a forwarding address. Or a telephone number.

"What are you doing here?" I breathed. "I didn't think you'd be in today."

Her chest lifted on a deep inhale, her lips parted, and then... "I was thinking I should probably come in and offer you an explanation," she murmured. "So you don't feel you have to look for me after I leave."

I jerked. Of all the things I'd thought she might say to me, that had never been on the list.

Still, I'd wanted answers. I wanted desperately to know who this girl was and how she'd come to be staying in her car outside of my office. And this, I supposed, was my chance.

I'd just have to deal with convincing her to change the leaving part later.

"Come to my office," I said quietly. "This isn't a conversation we need to have right there. In front of everyone."

Her eyes slid from mine to the room around her, and she blushed at all the eyes on us. Eyes that had already been wondering what was going on between us, I knew. Eyes that now saw me standing here holding her hand and begging her to come into my office. Eyes that could no doubt see that neither of us had slept last night.

I should have been embarrassed, too. After all, those were my employees out there making snap judgments about what Olivia and I were to each other, and I was sure the rumors would be flying within ten minutes.

I didn't care. I wanted to hear what this woman had to say, and I wanted a chance to change her mind about leaving.

"I'M SORRY FOR BREAKING your trust," I said immediately. It was the first, the most important thing to get out of the way. I knew I had, and I knew that I shouldn't have, and I wanted to make sure she knew both of those things.

She pressed her lips together, thinking. "Why did you do it?"

I lifted my eyebrows. "The truth?"

"Please," she said with a quirk of her lips. "I think it'll save us both an awful lot of time."

Right. The truth, then. "I wanted to know more about you," I said simply. "You wouldn't answer any of my questions, and even without knowing anything of your history, you're the most fascinating person I've ever met. I wanted to know... more."

Now it was her time to lift one dark, elegant eyebrow. "And you didn't think to... I don't know, ask?"

"I did," I pointed out. "Repeatedly. You didn't see fit to give me any answers."

Her eyes dropped toward the ground, her shoulders hunching in what felt like a defensive gesture. Something meant to protect her.

Something meant to close the rest of the world out.

I stretched out as quickly as I dared and took her hand from across my desk. I didn't know how Olivia worked, but I wanted to give her something. An anchor. An ally.

Someone to take with her. Someone she wouldn't have to run away from.

"Please tell me your name, at least," I breathed. "Give me that much."

Her eyelids fluttered... and then she looked up at me. "My last name isn't Cadwell," she breathed. "That's my mother's maiden name. I used it when I came here because I was running from someone. I needed to hide, and changing my last name was the easiest way to do that."

"And refusing to use any of your cards," I said, the details suddenly starting to fall into place. "Refusing to check in to a hotel. No wonder you were living in your car. And didn't have any money."

She tipped her head in what could have been an agreement, though I wasn't sure.

"Who were you running from?" I whispered.

No, I didn't know why I was whispering. It wasn't like anyone was going to hear us. We were alone in my office. But something about the moment, the situation, seemed to dictate quiet. And I wasn't going to argue with that.

She leaned forward, her arms on the desk and her eyes intense. "I can't tell you that."

I mirrored her pose. "Why not?"

Her face shuttered and closed at that question, and for a moment, I thought I'd lost her again. I thought she'd gone back behind that wall she was so good at building, never to tell me another thing.

But then I saw her narrow her eyes and bite her lip, like she was having an argument with herself. And a moment later, her face cleared again.

"I'm sorry," she said. "I'm not very good at sharing things about myself."

"Then just give me a piece," I told her carefully. "Give me a piece, and we'll go from there."

She laughed a bit. "Like it's just that easy." She pressed her lips together, though, starting to look... excited. And a moment later, she opened her mouth. "Parker," she said simply. "My last name is Parker."

I didn't dare to speak. It was so much more than I'd been expecting, and there was so much trust in her telling me that simple fact. Now I knew her real name, I was sure of it. Olivia Parker. And I knew what city she came from—or at least I thought I did—and I knew how old she was.

Telling me her last name was an incredibly big leap.

"And," she continued, "I left Sunnyvale because my mother's boyfriend threatened to kill me."

My blood, which had been so warm and sparkly a moment before, turned suddenly to ice water. "What?" I gasped, every hair on my body standing up on end and my muscles tensing with the sudden need to fight whoever had said that to her. "Why? What happened? What's his name?"

She put up a hand, laughing a bit. "You think I'm going to tell you that he threatened my life and then give you his name so you can go chasing after him? So you can get yourself into trouble? Not so fast, bub."

The laugh threw me off, but it had what I assumed was the desired effect. I let go of the tension I'd been holding on to and stopped thinking about slamming my fist into the face of whatever guy had threatened her.

And I started to see how stupid that reaction had been.

"Okay, that's fair," I said, giving her a wry smile. "But I think you at least owe me the story."

She sighed. "My mother... doesn't go for the nice guys. And this one is even worse than usual. I've always known he was a bad guy, but then I saw him actually hit her. I went to her immediately—once he was out—and told her that she needed to leave him. And of course, what does she do but run right to him and tell him that I told her so. Which led to him calling me and saying... well, some not very nice stuff. So I... left."

"Seems like the right call to me," I said, trying very hard to keep my voice light. "I mean, if someone threatened me, I'd choose leaving over staying any day."

She nodded, but it came with a cringe. "The problem is, I left my mom there with him. And I know he's probably gotten worse, because he's mad that I haven't shown up."

"And you can't save her unless she wants to be saved," I pointed out. "You have to protect yourself first, or you won't be able to do anything for her."

"I don't even know if I can protect myself," she said with a snort. "Why do you think I came here?"

I clutched her hand, which I now realized I was still holding, even harder. "Then let me protect you," I said. "Let me shelter you from him. I would be honored to serve as your bodyguard."

And though I thought it had been an incredibly generous thing to say—maybe even romantic—her face suddenly went... angry.

"Protect me?" she snapped. "You think you can just wave your magic money wand and make this all go away? Because I'll tell you what, Leo, it doesn't work that way. This guy, her boyfriend, is a nasty one, and I've known guys like him before. Money doesn't stop them. Privilege doesn't stop them. Nothing stops them except getting what they want. So no, I don't think you can protect me. But I think I can protect you. I can keep him away from you. Keep him from ever even knowing your name. But only if I leave."

She took a shuddering breath, her eyes growing suddenly colder. "That's what I came to tell you. I came to tell you the truth, and I came to tell you that I'm leaving. And it's for your own good, so please don't think you need to come after me."

She stood up and walked out while I was still trying to figure out how to make my voice work again.

And all I could do was sit there and watch her go.

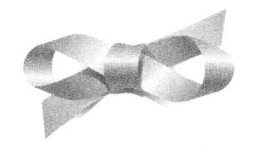

CHAPTER 3

OLIVIA

I HUSTLED DOWN THE hallway of the accounting department, my eyes on the door that led into my office, my brain refusing to believe what I'd just said to Leo in his office.

No, I hadn't meant to come right out with it like that. I definitely hadn't meant to leave immediately.

And even if I had, you'd better believe I'd wanted to do it in a nicer way than that. I'd come to care for Leo more than I was willing to admit, and even if I left...

When I left...

I wanted him to think that knowing me had been worthwhile. I wanted him to remember me fondly. Maybe even miss me.

I reached up and dashed away the tear that had built on my lower lashes, then swerved into my office and shut the door behind me, leaning back against it to give myself a moment to actually think and recover before I went back out there into the real world.

"Stupid," I huffed at myself. "Stupid, stupid, stupid."

What was I even so angry about? I reached into my brain, searching until I found the hot spot that Leo had touched, and looked closely at it. He hadn't done anything wrong. He'd just said that he could protect me. He'd offered to be my safe place.

And wasn't that what I'd thought in the beginning when I'd agreed to all of this? That he could be the safe spot I'd needed at that moment, when I was running for what felt like my life and didn't have any money or a place to stay?

So why had it set me off when he'd said it?

I narrowed my eyes and looked inward, searching for the reason, and gasped when I found it.

"Because it makes him sound like he doesn't think I can take care of myself," I said out loud.

I stepped forward, grabbed the laptop off my desk, and then turned and left the office, knowing that people were staring as I walked by, and knowing that they were staring because Leo and I had not only been holding hands in the office, but had also been fighting.

I didn't give one single fuck.

I wasn't going to be working in here much longer, anyhow, and I wasn't going to be working in here today. I was too angry—too hurt—to sit in my office and pretend that nothing had happened.

Leo didn't think I could take care of myself, and though somewhere deep down, I knew that I couldn't, not when it came to Roger, the idea that Leo would think that…

Well, it hurt a whole lot more than it had a right to hurt. And I wasn't going to sit in here with my heart breaking while he was right down the hall from me, not apologizing. I was going to get out of here, to a place where I could think and figure out how the hell I was going to get out of this newest mess.

I'd thought I would be able to get in and out with Leo. Spend the week with him, make the appearances he needed me to make, and then cut and run. I'd never meant for my heart to get involved.

I'd never thought I'd be getting so wound up over what the man thought of me that I could hardly see straight.

I'd certainly never expected to be second-guessing my need to leave before things got any messier, just because I didn't know if I could stand the thought of saying goodbye to him.

. . ~⚓~ . .

I SLUMPED BACK IN THE passenger's seat of my car—better because it had more space, thanks to the lack of steering wheel—and sighed.

"I don't know what I was thinking, Al. I don't even know if I was thinking at all."

"Sounds to me like you definitely weren't," she replied, not holding any of her punches. As usual. "Sounds to me like you were letting your emotions rule you. Gee, why does it feel like I've said this before…"

I snorted. "Probably because you've been saying it since we were kids."

"Probably," she said serenely. "Maybe one of these days you'll actually start to listen to me. Now, tell me again what happened."

So I told her. For the third time. I told her about dinner last night and how I'd been thinking that I didn't actually want to leave, even though I knew I probably should. I told her about Leo's phone call and our short and very intense conversation after that, and then I told her about the even more intense conversation this morning.

"So you told him who you are?" she asked breathlessly. "You actually told him?"

I banged my head back against the headrest. "Sure did."

"And you told him when you'd gone to Minneapolis?"

"Yep, told him that, too, because it turns out I'm complete shit at keeping secrets."

She paused for just a moment. "Or," she finally said, "you're finally figuring out how to tell people the truth."

I sat back up at that, scowling. "Hey, that's not fair. I know how to tell people the truth."

"Yeah. But not when you care about them. That one right there is a secret that you keep close to the chest every single time."

I bit my lip. She had me there.

It wasn't that I didn't want to tell people the truth about how I felt about them. When I realized that I felt something for someone—that

I wanted to take care of them and keep them safe and see them every single day—I wanted to tell them so.

Honestly.

But I'd grown up in a house where my dad had left my mother the moment he'd realized she was pregnant, and he'd never even bothered to meet me. My only memories of him were the times when my mom managed to get in touch with him to ask for help, and he'd been so horrible to her on the phone that she'd come away from the experience crying and told me that love wasn't all it was cut out to be.

My only experience with relationships, in other words, was that they were things that made one person cry and the other person disappear.

It had been a kid's view of them, yeah, and it was overly simplified and almost inevitably untrue. But I'd believed it for so long when I was a kid that it had sort of stuck. And I'd found myself in and out of relationships faster than you could say "scared of commitment," because the moment I realized that I had feelings—or that the other person did—I ran screaming in the other direction.

I didn't want to get caught in a situation like my mom had found herself in with my dad. I didn't want to feel trapped, and I didn't want to fall prey to having feelings for someone that the someone in question didn't return.

I never wanted to be that vulnerable. I never wanted to be that lost.

So I'd avoided them like the plague.

"You think I reacted the way I did because I care about him," I said.

It wasn't a question. I already knew the answer.

"Well, let's look at the facts," Alice said, her voice all logic. "You were crazy enough to get into a situation where you're literally living in the guy's house, and then you took a job at his company. You see him all the time. He buys you clothes and cooks you dinner. You've slept with him more than once, and you've gone out with him even when it wasn't required by your little contract. It hasn't been hard to hear you falling for the guy, Liv."

"But I wasn't going to let that matter," I said defensively. "In fact, I'm just trying to take care of him by leaving! It's safer for him if I leave!"

"Is it?" she asked softly. "Or is it just easier for you because that means you won't have to deal with the feelings?"

"Shit," I muttered. "Damn it, Alice."

"I love you, too, Liv," she said sweetly.

And then she hung up on me, the bitch.

Leaving me sitting in my car by myself with her words still ringing in my head—and causing all sorts of chaos inside my skull.

I'd known that leaving was the right thing to do because it would mean protection for Leo. I'd known that staying only meant giving Roger a straight shot at Leo, and I wasn't about to let that happen.

But Alice had, as usual, shown me the situation in an entirely different light. She'd seen it from outside of my head and pointed out the flaws in my plan.

The biggest flaw being that I wasn't really sure *why* I'd made the decision to go. *Was* it to protect Leo from Roger?

Or was it to protect myself from the feelings that I'd felt growing inside of me for the past week?

Was I actually running from Leo just because I was afraid of what he made me feel? Was that why I'd overreacted to him offering to protect me?

Because if it was... I wasn't sure it was a good enough reason to actually get into my car and start driving without a backward glance.

CHAPTER 4

LEO

I PRACTICED EVERY TRICK I knew to increase self-discipline that day, just to keep myself in the office.

Once I got over my paralysis and started thinking again, after Olivia walked out on me, I'd jumped up from my desk and darted to the door of my office, my head popping out into the hallway...

Just in time to see the woman in question emerging from the hallway on the other side of the floor, her eyes up and flashing dangerously at anyone who thought they were going to stop her and a laptop tucked under her arm.

I'd watched her charge from the hallway to the elevators, knowing that I couldn't go after her. She'd already said what she was going to say to me, and I had a feeling she wouldn't listen to anything else I wanted to tell her—or ask.

I also didn't think she'd thank me for making yet another scene in front of the cubicle swamp that took up the middle of this floor. People had already had an eyeful, and that was after all the coverage we'd had from the press at the charity auction.

If she was truly hiding, and if things in her hometown were as bad as she'd just told me, I didn't think she'd want to draw any more attention to herself than she had to.

I'd gone back into my office, feeling incredibly guilty about having put her in a bad position already, and spent the rest of the day telling myself every thirty seconds or so that I couldn't go after her. She'd taken her laptop, which I assumed meant she was working, and a quick check on the server showed me that she was, indeed, logged in.

That was going to have to be good enough for me for the day, I told myself.

I then proceeded to check the list of employees on the server every ten minutes or so to see whether she was still there.

And I didn't even feel guilty about doing it.

When I got home after the longest day in the history of long days, I walked into the kitchen and put my briefcase down on the counter, being as quiet as I could, my ears listening sharply for any sound in the house. Anything. Singing. Shuffling. Typing.

The sound of water running in a bathtub.

I turned my eyes from the door of her suite to the door of mine at that thought, a grin starting to grow on my face, but both doors were closed, and the hallway was dead quiet.

Shit, had she actually *left*? Had she come home, packed up her things, and gone without another word? Sure, she'd taken her work laptop and had been signed into the network all day, but she could have signed in and then left the laptop open.

I could have been looking at a ghost every time I checked that list.

I started toward her door, my heart hammering at the thought, and knocked three times when I got there. "Olivia?" I called softly. "Are you home?"

There was no answer, and I took that as enough excuse to open the door quietly, going very slowly so that if she was in there, she could run forward and stop me if she didn't want me coming in.

But there were no footsteps on the other side of the door. No palm slapped against a surface, no muttered demand that I mind my own business or stay out of her room.

Instead, the door opened on silent hinges, swinging into the room that I'd given Olivia to use as long as she stayed, my heart sinking lower and lower with every inch.

Because if she'd been in there, she would have stopped me by now. I was sure of it. And if the door was opening, it was because she wasn't in the house.

I let my eyes rake across the room, my heart in my mouth with fear of what I might see. A clean room. A made bed. No personal effects.

Instead... instead, I saw the closet half-open, showing hangers and hangers' worth of clothes, some of them turned inside out as though she'd been trying to figure out how they'd look on. A couple of pairs of shoes littered the floor, and the desk in the corner held a scattering of papers, plus several pens. Her bag was still on the floor, half unpacked, and I could see towels on the floor in the bathroom.

She wasn't gone, I realized, a rush of relief flooding through me. She was still... Well, she wasn't here, obviously, but she hadn't packed up her things and left.

And if she was going to leave without saying goodbye, today would have been the time to do it.

I slid back out of the room, closed the door firmly behind me, and took my phone out of my pocket, hitting the first number on my favorites screen.

I needed Jack, and I needed a drink. Several of them. Maybe if I drank enough and got enough advice from my best friend, I'd figure out how to make things right with Olivia. Before she decided to leave for real.

. . ༄ . .

"IF I'D KNOWN WE WERE coming here, I would have come right from the office," Jack muttered, sliding into the booth and pulling out a menu. "I'm starving. Hope you don't mind if I also get dinner."

I gave him a wave that said *Order whatever you want* and glanced out the window into the descending darkness. He was right, of course. My favorite bar was on the same block as the office, and it hadn't been the most efficient way to get a drink.

Still. The best pizza in town, combined with some truly genius beer choices and cocktails to boot, made it worthwhile, in my opinion.

"Considering I'm the one paying, I don't think you're in any position to complain about the ride," I said with a grin. "It's not like you drove yourself, after all."

Jack's face cracked into a smile. "Okay, well, when you put it that way..."

He looked up when the waitress arrived, gave her an appraising once-over, and then quickly ordered the biggest burger on the menu and his favorite craft beer.

"So dependable," I said, glancing back down at my own menu. "Always the same thing."

And then I proceeded to order exactly the same. Because tradition.

Jack just lifted his brows at me in silent judgment.

"Hey, when it works, it works," I said, shrugging. "I like the burgers here. What can I say?"

He tipped his head in consideration. "You can say why you needed to come out so badly, to start with. You can tell me what the hell's going on with you lately. And you can start with why you were checking the list of remote employees every five minutes today."

"Every ten," I corrected him. "Even I have some limits."

Another questioning look from him, another piece of silent judgment, and I sighed and jumped into the story. He was right. I needed to get this off my chest if I was going to figure out what to do about it.

I went through it all. Finding Olivia on the street—or rather, nearly being run over by her—and the idea that I could hire her to be my arm candy for the week to get the publicity team and the board off my back. The nights in with her, when we talked about everything from the news to the books we'd always wanted to read. Her taking baths in my tub when I was gone. The way she'd walked into my life and made herself a part of everything.

The news from the PI and her reaction to it. The threats to leave.

I didn't tell him that I'd slept with her. I also didn't tell him what she'd told me in the office, about her family or why she'd left Sunnyvale. Those things were private, and if I really wanted to win her trust again—if I wanted to be worthy of her trust—I knew I couldn't spread her personal information. Things that she hadn't even wanted to tell me.

There was also, to my surprise, a voice in my head telling me that if her mother's boyfriend was as bad as she thought he was, and if she was so worried that he'd be coming after me, then I needed to be careful.

I didn't want him coming after anyone else. Protecting Olivia herself was going to be hard enough.

Jack, to his credit, didn't question anything. He'd been there at the start of the entire plan, so he'd already known that part, and the rest, I supposed, was small potatoes compared to the fairly insane idea of hiring a girl off the street to be my date for the week.

He still, of course, found a way to locate the holes in my story and poke his finger into them.

"Why do you care so much if she leaves?" he asked finally.

Okay, that surprised me. "What?"

"Why do you care so much if she stays or goes? You were only contracted for the charity auction, right? That was all Meghan asked you to do? So what's the problem with just letting her go? She's held up her end of the bargain, and you've held up yours. Give her whatever payment you promised her and call it a day."

I didn't answer him, partially because the answer was way too complicated for me to go into over dinner and beers.

Partially because the answer wasn't only mine to give.

It had a whole lot to do with Olivia and the reasons she'd been living in her car in that alley... and a whole lot to do with the way it made me feel to think about her back in her car again and on the run without anywhere to go. It had even more to do with the solid idea that I could be her place to go. Well, my apartment could be her place to go.

It definitely all boiled down to the idea that I could be a safe haven for her. Protection. A base when she didn't seem to have one.

Add to that the way I was starting to feel about her—like she was the only face I wanted to see every day and the only person I could imagine sharing my nights with—and the whole thing was...

"I knew it," Jack said before I could finish that thought. "You don't want her to go because you have feelings for her."

That made my mouth drop right open, and I stared at him. "What?" I finally gasped.

"You have feelings for her," he said, shrugging. "There's no point in denying it, Leo. I've known you for a long time. I've seen you with a lot of girls, and I've never seen you this concerned about any of them before. You've known this girl for what, a week? And you're already holding on to her like she's the most important thing you've ever possessed. Damn, I thought you might actually stand up and walk out on the entire company when the board told you that you couldn't keep her."

"That's because they didn't have a good reason!" I pointed out, hearing how defensive I sounded even as I said it—and not caring.

They *hadn't* had a good reason. Just because she didn't have a degree, really? Just because we hadn't had a chance to do a thorough background check on her? It was ludicrous.

Jack got closer to me, his voice dropping and his eyes turning serious. "They had a very good reason, Leo," he said quietly. "You don't even know the girl's real name, and that means we didn't get a background check on her. She could be anyone. We don't know. And that's something you need to keep in mind. She might be beautiful. She might be brilliant. But you don't know what else she is. I don't think you can really commit anything to her until you have some answers."

I leaned back and reminded myself to keep breathing. I reminded myself that Jack didn't know what I knew about her.

And then I realized that just because she'd told me what she claimed was her background didn't mean she was telling the truth.

He was right. I didn't know who she actually was. I wanted to—badly. But until she got around to telling me the truth...

I was going to have to be very, very careful with my heart.

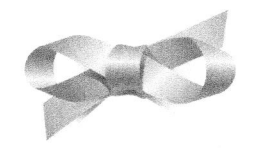

CHAPTER 5

OLIVIA

WHEN I WOKE UP, I'D been sleeping so hard that I couldn't remember exactly where I was.

Which was extremely disconcerting and more than a little bit scary.

I flipped my head back and forth, my gaze skipping over the room around me. Clean. Very expensive. Incredibly nice sheets. My stuff...

My stuff spread out across the floor and in the closet.

And then it came rushing back. Leo's apartment. I was in my suite in the apartment, sleeping in the same bed I'd been using for the last week. That was my closet right there—at least for the time being—and those were definitely my clothes, though he'd bought most of them for me, courtesy of the contract we'd agreed on.

I'd been here a week. I had to decide whether I wanted to stay any longer than that.

I'd been thinking about it all day yesterday while I worked on my laptop in my car, and I hadn't come to any solid conclusions. I'd worked all day and into the evening, though, and come home only after I thought he'd be asleep, just because I didn't want to talk to him. Not yet. Honestly, I didn't want to talk to him until I had an answer to my questions.

It wasn't exactly fair to put myself back in his orbit and then when he asked what I was doing, tell him I didn't know. Even I, who had such an issue with committing to things, knew that.

So where did that leave me?

"In a whole lot of crap," I grunted to myself.

The problem was, I didn't know how I felt about anything. Or rather... No, that wasn't quite true. I did know how I felt about things. I just didn't want to admit it—to myself or anyone else. Admitting it meant making it real, and making it real meant making it something that might tie me down and hold me in place.

Which was hard for someone who was used to running when things got tough.

So feeling as though I was actually falling in love with the guy? No, it wasn't new information. I'd known about it—or at least suspected it—for a couple of days. That didn't mean it was easy to deal with. And it didn't mean it was something I was going to start spreading around.

As far as I was concerned, it was no one's business but mine.

Still. It wasn't exactly the sort of thing that happened to you all the time, was it? It had never happened to me before, that was for sure.

"Facts, Liv," I told myself firmly. "Deal with the facts. Fact the first: he gave you a place to stay when you didn't have anyplace else to go. Fact the second: he promised you all the hot water you could use."

And from there, he'd bought me clothes and fed me and given me a job and a way to start believing in myself again, and...

And he'd kissed me like no one else had ever existed in the world for him and made love to me like it was the only thing he wanted to do. He'd made my body sing for him. And then he'd come back and done it again the next day.

Look, I hadn't had what you might call a good introduction to the world of relationships. I'd seen my own mother go through guy after guy, none of them treating her right and none of them bothering to stay around for long. I didn't trust the idea of committing to anyone else.

I knew how quickly they could leave you high and dry. I'd seen men do that to my mother too many times to blow it off.

I'd also never seen a single man care enough about my mother to buy her one damned thing. They certainly hadn't cooked her dinner or bought her fancy dresses or told her to take as many baths as she wanted.

I sighed and rolled out of bed, heading for the shower and trying to decide which side of my brain I wanted to listen to. The side that said all relationships were bad and were things to be avoided at all costs... or the side that said that Leo was unlike any man I'd ever known before, and that a relationship with him might just be... safe?

. . ⚘ . .

BY THE TIME I GOT OUT of the shower, I'd reached a compromise. I was in love with Leo. I hadn't wanted to admit it—even to myself—but there was no getting past it. I couldn't pretend that I didn't feel chills running through my body every time he came into a room, and I couldn't deny the effect his eyes had on me.

I definitely couldn't ignore the way every cell in my body seemed to be seeking him out at every second of the day, yearning for him in a way I'd never experienced before.

And I wasn't going to. For once in my life, I was going to listen to my emotions and my body rather than my brain and do something that made me feel good.

That didn't mean I was going to ignore my brain entirely, of course. I wouldn't have been able to, even if I'd wanted to. Instead, I'd found a compromise.

The perfect compromise.

"Stay another week," I whispered to myself, slipping into a pair of stockings and pulling them up my legs, being very, very careful not to snag them on anything. I stood up, adjusted the top to try to make it more comfortable, and then reached for the skirt I'd grabbed from the closet. "Stay another week, keep working, see how it goes. Stay another week, keep working, see how it goes. Stay another..."

I recited it to myself again and again, like some sort of talisman. A mantra that would keep me safe. Something to hold on to while I took this enormous leap of faith.

If it didn't work, I reminded myself, I could always leave. I knew I had an open-ended invitation to stay here. Leo wasn't going to kick me out unless I did something horrible to one of his first-edition books. I could stay here... and be safe.

With a roof over my head. And hot water. And food and company.

Company that included Leo himself.

It beat the hell out of leaving and living in some crappy hotel somewhere. By myself.

I straightened up and hooked the skirt closed, then met my own eyes in the mirror on the wall. "Stay here for another week. Give it a shot. See what happens. And if it doesn't work, I can leave then. Easy."

Or if not easy, at least solid. It meant I had a specific deadline, a specific goal. In a week, if things were still okay, I'd extend it another week. I could keep working.

Keep seeing Leo the way my heart was yearning to do.

I'd just have to keep Roger—and therefore my mother—at arm's distance so Roger didn't get any bright ideas about coming and looking for me and anyone I'd become friends with.

No problem.

Easy peasy.

．． ⚘ ．．

LEO HAD LEFT COFFEE in the coffee maker for me, and I took that as the evidence I needed that I was invited to stay in his life, at least for the time being—which was really all I wanted, anyhow.

One week. Then I'd decide again.

One week.

I took another sip of coffee, washed the mug out, and grabbed the bag I'd bought just for work, and then I was out the door. My laptop was still in my car, and that would give me a good excuse to actually drive to work rather than calling for a ride.

No, I wasn't taking my car because it might provide for a quick, clean getaway. What are you talking about?

Fifteen minutes later, give or take, I was parking in a parking spot in the alley where I'd first met Leo, my eyes on the diner across the street and my heart doing some sort of happy dance at the thought that I was going to see Leo in a few minutes.

"Stop it," I demanded. "Don't be stupid."

My heart, of course, didn't obey. Instead, the dance spread to my stomach as well.

I got out of my car, scowling at my inability to control my own organs, and walked quickly up the alley, past the corner where I'd almost hit Leo once—which still brought a smile to my face—and to the front door of the office. There, I stopped for long enough to stare at my reflection in the glass for several moments.

Not bad, I thought. The skirt was a good one, fitted in all the right places and extremely narrow around the knees, so it gave me an exaggerated hourglass figure. It was hell in a handbag to walk in, but the effect was well worth it, in my opinion. The blouse... also good, I confirmed, turning to the right and left to take myself in. The heels were amazing. Tall and yet somehow comfortable at the same time.

All in all, I actually looked like I *belonged* in an office like this.

That right there was going to take some serious getting used to.

I gave myself a nod, then pushed through the doors, the happy dance inside me turning into something a whole lot more nervous, like the fluttering of a million tiny wings.

I was actually nervous to see him. After the way I'd walked out yesterday and what I'd said...

I got into the elevator, my heart now thudding alarmingly, and hit the button for our floor. It was a quick trip, and by the time the door opened again, I had myself mostly under control.

My eyes, though, went straight to the door that belonged to Leo. The corner office that had a tiny hallway in front of it—just enough to make it appear isolated and not enough to actually hide it. He'd put the accounting department on the same floor, he said, because that was the most important department. The one that handled all the money and all the tricky stuff.

And he'd put me in charge of that department. On my word that I'd studied business and accounting in college.

Not exactly the actions of a man who was trying to screw you over. If only I could see that in my head.

If only that was the only thing I had to think about, an unwelcome voice reminded me.

It wasn't. I knew that. Roger and his goon squad were a much bigger threat. But knowing that Leo believed in me enough to entrust me with what he thought was one of the most important jobs in his whole company... Well, it meant something.

I left the elevator and made my way toward the hallway that contained my office—which took me in the opposite direction from Leo's. Every step hurt, every inch screaming that I should be heading toward him instead of away from him—if only because I owed him an apology—but I could already feel everyone staring at me, their eyes traveling up and down my body as they tried to figure out exactly who I was and how I'd gotten the job.

What I'd done to land it.

I firmed my lips and straightened up a bit, injecting pride into my posture. *I'm here, and I belong*, I tried to radiate. I had no idea if it was working, but no one was whispering as I walked by, and I figured that was a start.

When I first started, they hadn't been able to keep their mouths shut.

Not that I could blame them. For all they knew, I was sleeping with the CEO, and that was the only reason I'd been hired. Though I was hoping that my work over the last week had shown that I at least understood how to work with numbers.

If I stayed longer, I hoped that some of them would even start to respect me.

If.

· · ❦ · ·

"HEY, OLIVIA. I'M GOING downstairs for lunch. You want to come?"

I looked up from my computer, so surprised that I forgot how to use my voice, and just stared at her for far too long before I finally remembered that she was expecting an answer.

"Um, okay," I muttered. "I'm sorry, do we have a meeting or something?"

The woman, a pretty older woman with blond hair and laughing eyes, shrugged. "Not unless you want to. Honestly, I figured you were probably getting tired of people treating you like the local jezebel. Figured you might want someone who actually wanted to talk to you."

I laughed, caught off guard by her presence and that statement. "Yes," I said firmly. "I prefer Olivia to Jezebel, myself, and I could definitely use a friend."

She twittered in response, grinning like she'd just won some sort of lottery. "The cafeteria here is hit-or-miss, but I've heard they're doing sandwiches today, and you can order your own. Think it's worth the gamble?"

I hit the power button on my computer and stood up. "I have no idea. But I'm willing to give it a shot."

Hey, I'd just committed to staying here for another week. As long as I was going to do that, I figured I might as well start making some friends in the office.

And Sandy, who I recognized as the office gossip and the most outgoing employee on this floor, seemed like a terrific place to start.

CHAPTER 6

LEO

I KNEW OLIVIA HAD BEEN at the office, but only because I'd heard rumors about it. People whispering in the hallways about her presence there. Other people wondering whether she was going to stick. Others wondering what her background was—and still others defending her, pointing out that she'd fixed many problems in the accounting department in one short week.

I wanted to give the people who were defending her raises across the board.

I didn't, of course. Because that would have been... well, unfair. But it didn't change the fact that I wanted to cheer them on. More than that—I wanted to join in on those conversations and tell them how valuable she was, and how she was so smart that she'd learned the company's processes in the space of a couple of hours... and then improved them. Across the board.

She was worth a whole lot more than I was paying her.

Which was only one of the reasons I'd decided that I had to convince her to stay.

The others? Well, those were personal.

By the time I got out of the office, it was late, and I was both exhausted and hungry. I was also feeling nearly desperate to see the girl in question. Knowing that she'd been in the office all day, on the same floor as I was, though separated by so many cubicles I'd lost track of them, was... torture.

A sort of torture that I thought I could probably learn to enjoy, though. Torture that had kept me on the edge of my seat, my skin prickling with nerves all day—through meeting after meeting and phone call after phone call.

Now that I was finally heading home to the apartment I was hoping we still shared, I could feel the tension in my body rising. If things went the way I hoped they'd go, I would find her in my apartment when I got home, and it would be the first time I'd spoken to her since that meeting in my office, where she'd told me she was leaving.

She hadn't left yet. Could I do what it took to convince her to stay longer?

The tightening of my pants at the thought of her being in my house told me that I was counting on it. The rush of adrenaline through my body—most of it stopping in my crotch—told me that my brain agreed.

I liked the girl, and she was immensely talented. I wanted her to keep working for me, and I wanted her to keep living in my house. I liked knowing that she was there when I woke up. I liked even more the memories of the nights we'd spent together, our limbs tangled up and our skin pressed together.

I stretched in the back seat of my car, my joints suddenly languid with the memory of her body under mine, her eyes staring up at me as I pressed into her, her name on my lips. I closed my eyes and brought up a picture of her lying there, her hands over her head and her eyes taunting me as she waited. And another: her lying in my bathtub and muttering an apology—which was part accusation—for being there.

And I felt my pants growing even tighter, my cock coming quickly to attention with the memory of how she'd felt hovering over it.

And then I opened my eyes and sent those thoughts away, giving myself a very stern lecture about what I was about to walk into and how

I needed to handle it. The girl was scared and running from someone. She needed a safe place to stay and someone who would stand between her and the someone she was running from.

She did not need the guy she thought she could trust to walk into the apartment already hard and ready to take her to bed.

I growled at the thought, allowing myself one last flash of memory of her naked body, and then put it away.

If I was going to be her safe haven, if I was going to get her to trust me again, I had to learn to behave myself. Period. Because I wasn't willing to risk her actually leaving.

The car pulled up to my building then, and I clambered out, forgetting to wish my driver a good night in my haste to get upstairs to my apartment. The walk to the elevator took years, and the ride up to the penthouse took even longer.

By the time the elevator stopped, though, I'd succeeded in cooling my libido and calming my body down. When I stepped off the elevator and into the foyer of my place, I was cool, calm, and collected.

Until I walked through the library and living room and into the kitchen, where I found Olivia herself bent over and pulling something out of the oven. And damn, was she a sight to see. She'd changed out of whatever she'd worn to work and into some yoga pants and a tank top, and though these were probably more comfortable than whatever she'd been wearing before, they also showed every curve of her body, the pants clinging to her ass and the tank just a bit too tight.

How had I never noticed how toned her body was before? Was she some sort of fitness guru or something? Was that another part of the past she wouldn't tell me about?

She stood from the oven with something in her hand and turned, her eyes still on the dish she'd taken out, and slid it onto the counter. My eyes flicked down to see some sort of casserole—though I hadn't even known she could cook—and then flicked back up to see her sliding the oven mitt off her hand and blowing on her fingers.

At that point, her eyes came up to mine, and she jumped a bit. She hadn't known I was here.

"I'm sorry," I said quickly. "I didn't want to startle you while you had your head in the oven."

A smile flashed across her face. "I appreciate that."

She paused and bit her lip, a slight frown creasing her brow, and in that silence, I read her hesitation. She didn't know what she wanted to say to me. Or maybe... maybe she just didn't know how to say it.

"I'm sorry," we both blurted at the same time.

"I shouldn't have stuck my nose in—" I started at the same time as she said, "I shouldn't have said what I did—"

We both stuttered to a stop, caught in that awkward moment when you find you're speaking at the same time as someone else and both want to say what you started to... and hear what the other person was going to say.

"You first," I murmured, blood ringing in my ears.

"I'm sorry for saying that I was going to leave," she said breathlessly. "I'm sorry for getting so offended when you said you could help me. The truth is... I'm not good at this. I'm good at caring for other people but not at letting them care for me. I haven't exactly had a lot of practice at it."

"And I'm sorry for poking my nose in where it didn't belong," I returned quickly before I could lose my nerve. "I'm sorry I didn't just give you time to tell me yourself. Please don't go. Please stay. If you stay, I promise to give you as much time as you need when it comes to telling me things. I promise to have better patience."

That won me a much brighter smile, her face lighting up with something that looked a whole lot like relief. "Really?" she whispered. "You want me to stay?"

"More than I've ever wanted almost anything in my entire life," I confirmed.

Instead of answering, she walked quickly toward me, slid her hands up my neck and around my jaw, and kissed me, the kiss starting out sweet and questioning... and turning quickly hotter.

I hadn't been expecting it, but that didn't mean I was going to throw it away. I threw the bag I'd been carrying to the floor, out of the way, and wrapped my own hands around her back, clenching her shirt there in my sudden, overwhelming need to have more of her. To have everything.

I'd very nearly lost this girl, or at least I felt as though I had. The idea that she was staying—and was so happy about it—brought my desire screaming back to life, my body heating so quickly I was surprised I didn't spontaneously explode. I kissed her deeply, my tongue dancing with hers in that breathless, timeless moment when we both realized that we weren't going to have to say goodbye. And when she groaned against me, half satisfaction and half need, I knew we were going to go a whole lot further than just kissing.

And if I'd thought my cock was hard before, it was nothing compared to what it became now. Every ounce of blood in my body went rocketing right to my crotch, my cock straining at the zipper of my pants in its need to be freed.

I broke the kiss and looked down at Olivia. "Are you sure?" I gasped. I didn't know what I was going to do if she said no, but I knew I had to give her the option. I'd told her I would respect her from here on out.

That meant making sure she was sure about what we were doing right now.

She reached up and tugged my lower lip down with her thumb, her tongue darting out between her teeth as she watched her own actions. And when her gaze came back up to mine, it was burning with desire.

"Positive," she whispered. "Take me to bed, Leo. I want to remember what it feels like to have you."

She didn't have to ask me twice. I slid one hand under her ass and the other behind her back and scooped her up, never taking my eyes off of hers, and made directly for the bedroom.

. . ∽ . .

"LET ME GET SOME OF these clothes off," I whispered, setting her on the bed. I turned and began stripping quickly out of everything I had on—tie, jacket, shirt, slacks—and the tension inside me grew with each moment, until I felt like a spring that had been compressed too tightly. My muscles coiled, desperate for release, and my cock was a throbbing, aching thing now, every moment riding a fine line between pleasure and pain.

When I was finally nearly naked and turned around, I found Olivia already stripped and lying in bed, watching me.

Hot damn, the woman was beautiful. Curling brown hair, eyes so bright a blue that they almost hurt to look at, and the face of an angel.

With the attitude of a demon, I reminded myself firmly.

My demon. My argumentative, opinionated, stubborn girl. Or if not mine, yet... then at least staying.

I growled at the sight of her and crawled into bed, making my way over her body and spreading her legs slowly with my own.

"Are you ready for me?" I asked, knowing that I wasn't going to have the patience for foreplay tonight. I'd wanted this too much for the last two days to be able to stand any delay.

"Readier than you could possibly know," she answered.

She lay back on the pillow, her eyes on mine, and reached up to my face, cupping my jaw and guiding me forward to kiss her while her other hand went to my cock and began to stroke me. I gasped and spasmed, surprised, and reached down to stop her.

The moment my hand touched hers, though, she guided me forward, moving me until the tip of my cock was nudging at her opening.

"Fuck," I gasped.

"Oh yeah?" she asked, a sly smile creeping across her face. "I wasn't aware you couldn't handle this."

I growled in response.

She pulled a bit harder, sliding my head between her folds and inside her, and then it was far, far too late to stop and talk any further. I grabbed her hand and held it out to the side, moving her other hand to match and spreading her for me, and slid home, groaning as the pleasure raced through my body and came to a point just there, where I felt her wrapping around me and welcoming me.

And then I slowly pulled out... and pushed back in, knowing that we had all night, and that this time, I was going to make love to her.

This time, I was going to show her how good it could be if she stayed.

CHAPTER 7

OLIVIA

I DIDN'T WANT TO OPEN my eyes the next morning when I finally came back to consciousness.

I didn't want to let the night—and all that had happened in it—go, and I certainly didn't want to return to the real world, where things like the office and expectations and villains awaited me.

Instead, I snuggled back against the man that I got to keep for another week, sighed happily, and allowed myself to drift away in a spot between asleep and awake, my mind on the night we'd just spent together.

Of course, nothing can last forever, and it felt like about five minutes before Leo's alarm started going off, telling him that it was time to come out of the hazy, dreamy spot we'd created and enter the real world again, by way of his office.

"Can't you call and tell them you're not coming today?" I asked sleepily. "And while you're at it, tell them that I also won't be in."

His arms surrounded me and pulled me back against him, the hard length of him sliding between my legs and rubbing against my clit in a way that made me gasp and squirm.

"Pretty sure it would start rumors if I called in and included you on that particular account," he murmured against my neck.

"Can't you tell the entire office not to come in, then?" I asked on a gasp when his movements became more determined. "Give everyone a day off, and they won't even know we're taking one. You're the boss, right?"

"Boss enough to know I can't afford for the entire company to shut down for the day," he returned. "Though I think we can probably be late, at the very least."

His hands went to my hips, and he moved me slightly, repositioning me against his cock.

I cried out when he entered me, sliding up to the hilt against flesh so sensitive that I could barely stand it.

"Do you want me to stop?" he growled.

Instead of answering, I arched my back, bringing my pelvis up and changing the angle slightly. Until the pain turned into something so good that I could barely breathe.

Leo's growl turned deeper and darker then, his fingertips firmer against my skin, and he pulled me back against him again. "Or do you like it like this?"

He started moving me, sliding his cock in and out with plenty of friction ending up further south, and I gasped. Damn, that was good.

Damn, it was—

"I might," I answered him, hearing my voice come out in a sultry, sexy impression of my usual daytime tone.

"Oh, you just *might*?" He made as if he was going to pull out, leaving me until only the tip was still inside me, and I panicked, pushing back against him. His hands were there, though, stopping me from moving, and I nearly cried out in sudden emptiness at the feeling.

"I do," I gasped, aching for more. Burning for him.

And suddenly he was back, slamming into me again and then turning me on my stomach, his body between my legs and my eyes staring into the mirrored headboard. I turned my gaze up to his and saw his face creased with sleepy desire, his eyes burning for me as he tipped my hips once again so he could get deeper and then fucked me from this new angle, his eyes burning hotter and brighter the longer we went.

LEO POURED ME ANOTHER cup of coffee and then grinned at me in a way I already knew was going to mean trouble.

"So I've been meaning to talk to you about something," he started. "There's a fancy corporate dinner tonight, and I'd like you to go with me."

"A corporate dinner that you need a date to?"

"A corporate dinner that I don't need a date for, but that I want to take you to," he corrected. He finished pouring and shot me an even naughtier grin. "It's at a very fancy restaurant. And between the two of us, I'm sure we'll be able to cook up an excuse to leave early."

I tipped my head in consideration. "So a fancy restaurant that you don't want to stay at too long. I have to say, that's not selling me on the idea."

"It'll mean you get another dress."

I snorted at that. "I don't need another dress. I already have one."

"But you can't exactly wear that again. People have already seen it. Think of it as getting to spend more of my money."

"I don't actually enjoy spending your money, believe it or not," I told him, rolling my eyes.

He rolled his eyes back. "But will you come? Will you save me from the boredom of eating out with all of those people who have nothing in common with me?"

I had to laugh at the desperation in his voice—and the picture of him as the poor victim, here, who needed saving. And in the end, I did agree that I'd go with him—and that I would, under duress, buy another dress.

The smile he gave me when I said so was nearly worth the headache I knew it was going to be going shopping again. On my lunch break. With an expectation of finding a dress immediately.

"I KNOW THE PERFECT place," Sandy said when I told her. "They only deal in dresses, and they have stuff so gorgeous you'll practically orgasm for it."

I snorted with laughter at that. "I'm pretty sure orgasming all over the dress would ruin it. Maybe I'll save that for later."

She lifted one very blond, very elegant eyebrow, like she was having all sorts of thoughts about what I might mean by that, and I immediately regretted saying anything. There was already enough gossip about Leo and me in the office. I didn't need to add to it myself.

I wondered, though, how much of that gossip Sandy actually knew—and how much she'd been responsible for. The woman could have been a reporter for the biggest magazine around with as much as she knew about the people in the office, and I didn't doubt that she'd been involved in at least one conversation where she speculated about what my relationship was with Leo and whether that had helped me to land my job.

I wasn't going to ask her, of course.

Well, not yet. Later, when we knew each other better?

Probably.

For right now, though, I needed a dress, and if she knew a place that might be a good option, I was going to go for it.

"You're an angel," I told her, relieved. "And I'm dragging you with me. Leo's promised a long lunch, and I'll need advice. I'm really, really bad at shopping."

Her eyes dragged up and down my body, which was clad today in a bright red business suit complete with black blouse and heels.

"You don't *look* like you have trouble shopping."

"Believe me, I only look this good because I had help," I assured her, remembering Linda, who'd come to the apartment with half of her store's stock and told me that the more I bought, the better her commission would be.

I felt a thrill of warmth at the thought and reminded myself that I needed to call her. Linda had been my first friend in Minneapolis and was also incredibly bright. We'd gone to the same university—though we hadn't known each other there—and had majored in nearly the same thing.

In fact, I sort of hoped that whatever store Sandy was talking about was the one Linda worked at. The woman had been a godsend when it came to shopping for clothes.

It turned out that this was a completely different place, though, and when Sandy and I had strolled into the store down the street from the office, I'd looked around, shocked at all the glamor. I'd thought the clothes Linda had brought were expensive.

They didn't look like they held a candle to what they sold here.

"Are you sure we can afford this?" I asked, looking around in awe.

"Are you shopping with Leo's credit card?" she returned.

I blushed all the way from my chin up to my hairline. Was I allowed to admit that sort of thing? Then again, I had told her that Leo had given me a long lunch break specifically for this shopping trip, so it wasn't like his involvement was a secret.

"Sure am," I told her, a grin starting to peek out.

She nodded. "Then you'll do just fine here. I've always dreamt of buying something here, but I've never been able to manage it." She gave me a saucy, very triumphant grin. "But I'm on board with helping you spend *his* money. He's a great boss, but he's never going to notice the cost of a dress. Let's go."

She grabbed my hand and towed me into the shop, and before long, we had two salespeople tottering after us, their arms full of dresses and shoes and even underwear that Sandy wanted me to consider.

Personally, I didn't think we needed all of that. But I was too excited about having a friend here shopping with me to tell her no.

And when I started added clothes for her to try on, too, and asking her what sort of dress she would buy for herself, her grin—and my feeling of finally belonging somewhere—just got bigger.

Not that I wasn't worrying. Yes, I'd agreed to stay with Leo for another week—at least in my head—and yes, I thought that would probably be fine. As long as we were careful.

But a corporate dinner, where there was bound to be more press and at least a reporter or two? It was even more opportunity for someone to catch me in a picture and then publish it on a site where Roger might see it. Also dangerous: the idea that the people there would be asking me questions and trying to get to know me.

They'd know I worked for the company. They'd know what I did and how I'd come to be in the job. And they'd be asking about my qualifications and what I'd done in the past.

I'd managed to blow past Leo's questions and keep mostly to myself in the office, and that had been working just fine for me. But when it came to being trapped in a dinner, with so many people asking questions...

How long was I going to be able to maintain the ruse of being one person before I did something to mess it all up? And what would Leo do when it all came tumbling down?

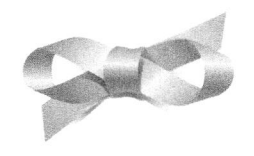

CHAPTER 8

LEO

I DIDN'T SEE OLIVIA again during the day, and by the time I got home, she was already locked in her room (theoretically, though I didn't check the door to be sure), and I could hear the shower running. I glanced at my watch, suddenly panicked that I was running late, and saw that we still had around two hours before we were due to leave for the dinner.

She was running ahead of time, then. Though given how nervous she'd been when I saw her at lunch, I wasn't surprised. She'd agreed to come to this dinner with me—and buy the dress—but her face had told me very, very clearly that she didn't want to.

I wondered what it was that had her so nervous... and then I turned to my own room. I doubted I would take as long to get ready as she did—no makeup or hair to do, after all—but I also hadn't seen the suit I was planning to wear tonight in a couple of months.

I'd better make sure it was still all there, or I was going to run into trouble myself.

BY THE TIME I LOCATED all pieces of the suit in question—including the tie I liked to wear with it, which had gone missing and took me ages to find—got through my own shower, did what I could with the mess of curls on my head, and got into my shoes, I was feeling pretty thankful that we'd started getting ready so early.

Or rather, that Olivia had started getting ready so early. If she hadn't, I wouldn't have, and then I would have been in a real bind.

Just another example of her somehow saving me without seeming to do anything other than existing.

The thought made me pause in tying my shoe, and I bit my lip, trying to wrap my head around it. The girl had been in the right place at the right time more than once, and beyond that, had managed to have the right skills to solve a problem precisely when I needed them.

I wasn't a big believer in fate—and never had been—but it was getting awfully hard to ignore the way she was changing my life, lighting it up in a way no one had ever done before.

The fact that she was doing it when I still didn't know who she was or whether she might stay made that a distinctly uncomfortable thought. I didn't particularly like the idea of having someone light up my life and then disappear into the mist.

Which, I had to admit, I was still very afraid she might do.

I shuffled into the hall, that thought foremost in my mind, and came to a screeching halt.

Because I might be worried that Olivia would disappear like dust in the wind at any point, but right now, in the hallway, the girl standing before me was 100 percent real. Or at least I thought she was.

Though if someone had told me she was a vision pulled from my own imagination, I wouldn't have argued with them.

She was beautiful. Beyond beautiful, though I didn't know the word for it. She'd found a formfitting gown in the exact same color as her eyes, the material shimmering somewhere between blue and green, and changing as she checked her reflection in the hallway mirror, and though the color might have washed anyone else out, it was somehow making her cheeks look rosier, her hair darker, her lips more…

"Perfect," I whispered.

She jerked her gaze from the mirror to me, her mouth open in surprise. "What? What is? My hair? I didn't know what to do with it, so I just left it down. Is it going to be too... casual?"

I grinned. Her hair was indeed mostly down, the curls cascading down her back and over her shoulders in a waterfall of chocolate brown touched with auburn.

"No, your hair is perfect," I assured her. "Unless..."

I moved toward her, drawn like a moth to a flame, and moved behind her to brush her hair to the side, exposing her neck. Then, following the same instinct that had brought me to her side, I leaned down and ran my lips along the curve where her shoulder met her neck.

"Yes, this works very well, I think," I breathed.

She shuddered at the feel of my touch on her skin, her chin tipping up a bit as she breathed out.

She did not, I noticed, move away from me to keep me from touching her. Which made me think that the newly physical aspect of our relationship just might stick. Maybe she wasn't as close to leaving as I feared.

Maybe she was feeling the same things I was feeling.

"Do that again and we're never going to get out of this apartment," she finally said, her voice colored with both desire and laughter.

I pressed another kiss to her shoulder, this one firmer. "I don't think that would be the worst thing in the world."

And now she did snort and step away from me, turning smoothly so she was facing me and tipping her chin up even more. "I thought you said this dinner was important enough that I had to buy a dress for it! If it's not, why did I have to go shopping?"

I rolled my eyes. "You know, most women would jump at the chance to go shopping at every opportunity."

"I guess I'm not most women, then."

She certainly wasn't. Not that I was going to tell her that.

"Unfortunately, you're right. The dinner is important. We can't skip it. The entire corporate suite is going to be there, and that means I have to put in an appearance. But—" I grabbed her wrist when she was about to turn away and pulled her back, dropping my voice to a throaty growl. "I'm counting on you to give me a very good reason to leave early. And when we get home, I'm not planning on going right to sleep."

Too much? I wasn't sure. I did know that I wanted to tell her how I was feeling about her. But when it came to talking to women...

Well, I'd always been more concerned with the company than I was with dating—which Meghan had been so keen to remind me of when this whole thing started.

Fortunately, Olivia didn't seem put off by my suggestive statement. Instead, she lifted a brow and quirked her mouth to the side. "Not going right to sleep? What are you going to do, stay up and play Nintendo all night or something?"

I was so surprised that I actually jerked.

I might not have been good at dating. But Nintendo? I'd been playing it since I was a kid. It was, in fact, one of my secret and very hidden obsessions.

"Nintendo?" I asked, my voice overly casual. Way too innocent to be truthful. "I don't know what you're talking about."

She did a little shimmy with her shoulders, telling me that she knew that I knew exactly what she was talking about. "And you, Leo, are a liar. I saw the setup in your room. I know you must play at night by yourself." She leaned forward and widened her bright, beautiful eyes. "I know how many games you have."

We could have been talking about the sexiest thing I'd ever done in my life based on her voice, and my pants were growing tighter every second with her presence. That sexy voice. The way she was dropping her shoulders and allowing the dress to slide down her chest a bit, exposing more skin.

Wait, what was the question?

"And what's your point?" I asked, my voice hoarse.

She chuckled, her own voice throaty and incredibly sexy. "My point, Mr. Folley, is that I know your secrets. I know what you do at night when you're by yourself, and if you're going to come home early but not sleep, I can only guess that you're going to be attached to that system in your room, playing whatever your newest obsession is."

My newest obsession was her.

And I knew I couldn't say that.

I also hadn't planned to come home to play Nintendo. But as long as that was what she thought I was going to be doing…

"And do you play?" I asked, injecting plenty of suggestion into the question.

She giggled. "Do I play Nintendo? Probably not the way you do. But I've been known to pick up a controller from time to time."

"Then it's a date," I told her firmly. "After an hour at the dinner, we find an excuse to leave. And then it's game on."

She agreed, still grinning, and then I took her hand and led her out of the apartment, my mind already skipping right through the dinner and to what we were going to be doing afterward.

· · ⚜ · ·

ONCE WE GOT TO THE dinner, of course, my nerves kicked back in. This wasn't only a dinner for the corporate club, but also for the investors in the company, which meant the board would be there with all their judgments about Olivia and how suitable she might or might not be as an employee. And as my date.

Honestly, if I'd had any sense, I wouldn't have brought her. But I was growing to like having her by my side at important events, and I was surprisingly interested in hearing her opinion about some of the team.

No matter what anyone said about the woman, she had one of the brightest minds I'd ever met, and she definitely knew how to read people. I wanted her on my team for that reason alone.

There were other reasons, of course. But for tonight, she was here as my eyes and ears and mouth.

And the best part was that I wouldn't even have to tell her that. I knew her well enough now to know that she'd observe and report just as part of her personality. She was the ideal partner.

As long as I could get past the idea that she might leave without telling me tomorrow.

When we walked in, every head in the room swiveled toward us, and I knew it wasn't because I was there. No, all eyes were on Olivia, and I knew what they had to be seeing. A drop-dead gorgeous woman holding her own next to me, and the girl who I'd hired to oversee the accounting department. A girl who had, furthermore, revolutionized many of the processes in that department and cleaned up the efficiency already.

A girl who was already saving us money.

I didn't know if they'd all be seeing that, though. I thought it far more likely that they'd be seeing the girl I was dating and had given a job to. The girl who hadn't earned it for herself.

It was going to be a tough crowd tonight. I just hoped Olivia was up to the challenge.

Unfortunately, those challenges started almost immediately. One of the lead investors slid up to us, all oily smoothness and toothy smile, and held a hand out to Oliva. "You must be the genius accountant I've been hearing so much about."

She smiled and took his hand, though I could see a hitch in her smile that told me she wasn't entirely pleased about the way he'd introduced himself. "I suppose I am, though I certainly don't like to brag about it."

He chuckled as though he was doing her a favor by laughing at her little joke. "And also dating our Leo here. Showing him a good time, are you?"

My skin began to burn with fury at his tone of voice and the implications of what he was saying, but Olivia took it in stride, her shoulders growing firm and her back straightening a bit.

"I don't believe it's actually my job to show him a good time, Mr....?"

She arched one brow, waiting for him to give her his name, and he twitched.

"Burns," he said quickly. "Ed Burns."

"Mr. Burns," she continued smoothly. "My job is to make sure the company keeps the money it makes. I'm sure you can understand how important that is, being an investor. After all, you wouldn't want to see the department in the hands of someone who didn't know what they were doing, would you? And I believe my results already speak for themselves."

I turned my eyes from her to Burns, trying very hard to keep the smile off my face at the way she'd just put him in his place, and saw that he'd grown at least a shade paler.

He probably wasn't used to having anyone speak to him that way, least of all a woman he'd thought he could embarrass.

But he'd never met Olivia.

He turned from her without replying and dropped his voice. "I need to meet with you on Monday, Folley. Go over some important thoughts on personnel."

I nodded and muttered something about him calling my assistant to book the time, then took Olivia's hand and moved into the room. She squeezed my hand supportively, and I squeezed back, already knowing exactly what Burns was going to say and doing some rapid calculations in my head.

If he was going to have a problem with Olivia working there, he'd find that I wasn't likely to listen to them. And if he decided to pull out, I wasn't going to stop him.

I had enough money to cover his portion of the company. I wasn't concerned about that.

But I didn't want Olivia hearing that I might lose investors because of her. She was already far too close to leaving for my liking, and I didn't want her getting it into her head that doing so would protect me.

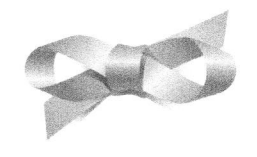

CHAPTER 9

OLIVIA

I GOT INTO THE KITCHEN the next morning with my eyes feeling like they were only half working from too little sleep and too much to drink at dinner the night before. Now in the morning light, it seemed insane to me that Leo had thought it was a good idea to host a big fancy dinner on a weeknight.

Even more insane, honestly, that we'd both thought it was okay to come home from said dinner and continue drinking while playing Nintendo until the wee hours of the morning.

I woke up this morning deeply questioning not only that idea but also our ability to be responsible adults. My head felt like someone was trying to jackhammer through it from the inside, and though my stomach seemed relatively stable, I definitely wasn't going to challenge it with anything too daring today.

I was very surprised, therefore, to find a note taped to the coffee maker from Leo, saying that he'd not only already gotten up and headed for the office, but that he'd made coffee cake and it was in the oven staying warm.

I snatched the note up and looked at it more closely, trying to see whether it said what I thought it said. It did. No matter how many times I read it, it definitely said that he'd gotten up early, made coffee, baked, and then headed for the office before I'd even opened my eyes.

"What did he do, not sleep at all?" I asked, frowning.

Not that I minded. I hadn't wanted anything risky to eat. But coffee cake sounded completely safe, if you asked me. I also wasn't going to complain about someone else having made it before I was even awake.

I did, though, start making a list in my head of the reasons that Leo might have gone into the office so early. Reasons that would have included him not saying anything to me about it last night—or leaving anything more than a note about coffee cake.

I didn't come up with anything that I thought was worthwhile during my shower. Or my breakfast. Or the ride to the office itself. When I did arrive, though, I heard within thirty seconds that Leo was in a mood and that it would be better to avoid his office for the day—a message delivered by the ever-helpful Sandy. I paused in my doorway and cast a glance at Leo's office, which was currently closed.

Then I told myself that I'd keep an eye on the office this morning and call that good enough.

After all, if Leo was in a mood about something, it wasn't my job to try to figure out what it was—or take care of him. He wasn't my husband. Or boyfriend. Or dad. He was just a guy whose apartment I was staying in while we completed a contract that called for me to be his arm candy. He was also the guy who was currently playing my boss, if you wanted to count that, though even then, it was just because I was doing him a favor.

I was only here until he found someone else to take over. I was only here for another week. After that, I'd be long gone—and I wouldn't have to worry ever again about whether he was in a bad mood or not.

That particular conclusion didn't make me feel as good as I was hoping it would, though. Instead, it left a sort of hollow feeling in the pit of my stomach.

The idea that his mood might have a whole lot to do with him thinking that he'd been spending too much time around me, a girl he didn't mean to keep around, made that pit a whole lot deeper.

The problem was, I couldn't ignore that last point. If I was going through life reminding myself every five minutes that I was only going to be here for another week, and that I didn't have to care about someone who was only going to be in my life that long, then what was *he* doing? Because I rather doubted that he was making long-term plans when it came to me.

Which meant that he probably wasn't all that happy about having stayed up all night playing Nintendo with yours truly. A girl he didn't mean to keep for much longer.

A girl he had to know didn't mean to stay for much longer.

"Ugh," I moaned, letting my head drop onto my desk. These sorts of thoughts were too much to handle on an early morning, slightly hungover stomach.

I needed numbers. Numbers always acted the way you thought they should and never changed their spots in the middle of a calculation. They didn't suddenly start acting differently than they should, and they definitely never had—or depended on—emotions.

They were safe. Dependable. Consistent.

And with that thought in mind, I dove into the nearest spreadsheet, turning my mind resolutely away from Leo and whatever was causing his mood and toward the problem of tracking individual employee spending accounts in a more efficient way.

At least there was a solid answer to that problem. Hopefully one I could come up within the next hour or so.

. . ⚜ . .

BY LUNCH, I HAD SUNK myself so deeply into my numbers that I'd nearly forgotten about Leo and his mood. Two steps out of my office, though, and I remembered. Leo's door was open now, and I could see him sitting at his desk, his face creased with concern and frustration—directed, I assumed, at the man who was sitting opposite him. I watched Leo listening and nodding and then saying something back to the anonymous man.

A moment later, they both stood up and shook hands, though judging by Leo's face, it wasn't a friendly sort of shake. The stranger—who had now turned around and was walking out of the office—was an older guy that I'd never seen before, though he had "rich" written all over him, and it didn't take much to guess that he was a money guy.

Leo, though, didn't look like the man had offered him any money. Instead, he looked like the guy had just pulled the rug right out from under him. He saw the man through the door of his office and then watched him walk toward the elevators, his eyes narrowed and his lips pressed into a thin line.

Then he turned and saw me watching him.

I ducked back around the corner and out of sight. Yes, I knew that he'd seen me. But I also knew that I wasn't sure how I wanted to handle the situation. Go and comfort him in regard to whatever had just happened? Look away and pretend that I hadn't seen anything—and worse, that I didn't care, even if I had?

Getting out of sight and putting it off for later was a better idea, as far as I was concerned. It meant not making any decisions right now—which meant not having to consider how I felt about the man and what I might want to be to him beyond just the girl he'd found living in her car, who was a convenient piece of arm candy.

After all, arm candy wouldn't need to have feelings for the man who had been playing white knight. Arm candy could just enjoy the hot water and the food, then take the money and run.

I spent the rest of the day playing dumb about the whole thing and sticking close to my office just so I didn't have to make any snap decisions about how to handle the Leo question.

When I got home, though, and found him sitting in the library with his head in his hands, looking like he'd just had the worst day ever,

I couldn't stand it anymore. No, I didn't want to save him, and I certainly didn't want him to think he could count on me—because that would make it even more awkward if I had to leave—but you can't just walk right past a man who's obviously so miserable and not do anything to try to help.

I mean, you probably *could*. But I didn't have a heart made of ice.

I let my bag slip through my fingers, walked over, and dropped to my knees in front of him.

"Well, you don't look good," I observed casually.

I heard a quick breath that could have been a laugh if he'd put more effort into it. "I don't feel that great, either."

"Head hurting?" I asked. "Because I've got to tell you, today was one hell of a day with the headache I have."

He tipped his head up and gave me a very wry smile. "The headache definitely hasn't helped."

"You know what I've always found to be a cure for headaches?" I asked, skipping right past all the other things that might have made today rough on him.

"Sleep?"

I made a face. "I mean sure, sleep, but where's the fun in that? You can do that any old time, right?"

He made a face back at me. "I suppose so, though it's all I wanted all day, and yet I didn't get it. What do you have that's better?"

I tilted my face up and gave him the big eyes. "Ice cream," I whispered. "And I don't come from this city, but someone at work was telling me about an ice cream shop right down the street from here. One of those places where you can design your own and then eat it there. The place is supposed to be done up all old-fashioned, like a Parisian shop or something. Sounds like the perfect sort of place to let the real world go and just enjoy life for a second. What do you think?"

His shoulders dropped at least an inch, and I could see the tension almost melting out of him. "And you think it'll help get rid of the headache?"

I stood and held out my hands. "I don't think it'll make it any worse, and it'll keep you from sitting here pouting on your own. Seems like a double win to me."

"Double win it is," he murmured, sliding his hand into mine and letting me pull him up.

• • ⚜ • •

THE ICE CREAM PARLOR was everything I'd heard it would be, complete with red leather in the booths, a black-and-white tile floor, and fanciful chandeliers overhead. One entire wall was a counter full of different ice cream flavors and toppings with several people taking orders, scooping, and mixing, and the entire place had that bright, cheerful sort of lighting that you generally only see in places that cater to kids.

"See?" I asked, my hand still in Leo's and our bodies pressed together. "A whole different world. Definitely nothing real about this place."

"You think the calories are pretend, too?" he asked, eyeing the ice cream. "Because I think I might need three scoops."

I leaned toward him and brought my mouth up to his ear. "I'm pretty sure you could order five scoops, and no one would judge you."

I caught the gleam of his eye as he grinned down at me, and then it was our turn.

"Three chocolate scoops and two mint," he told the girl on the other side of the counter. "With chocolate sprinkles and chocolate chips mixed in."

I snorted. "If you're going to go for that much ice cream, I figured you'd at least get creative about it."

He looked shocked at that. "I'll have you know that mint chocolate chip is quite possibly the best flavor combination ever invented!"

"Not even close," I told him with an airy wave. When I turned back to the girl in charge of taking my order, I was grinning. "I'll take one scoop of raspberry sherbet, one scoop of chocolate, one scoop of cake batter, and two scoops of cheesecake, please. Chocolate chip cookie dough and Twix for the toppings."

When I looked at Leo, I found him staring at me like I'd just started speaking Greek.

"What?" I asked innocently. "Too much for your brain to take in all at once? And here I thought you were creative."

CHAPTER 10

LEO

"CAN I GET YOU TO DO me a favor?" I asked, standing in the doorway of Olivia's office and praying that she'd say yes.

She looked up from her computer, looking about one hundred times better healthier than she had the last time we were in the office. Of course, the last time we were in the office, we'd very stupidly just spent nearly an entire night playing video games and drinking rather than sleeping.

I would have been worried if she'd looked that bad after she'd had an entire weekend to recover.

"Sure," she said immediately. "What's up?"

A small part of the tension in my shoulders released at her quick agreement, though I could still feel the rock sitting in the bottom of my stomach.

"I'm going into a meeting right now, and it would make my life a whole lot easier if you'd go into it with me."

Her mouth twitched. "What am I, your security blanket now?"

My mouth twitched in response, though I wasn't even close to laughing. "Not exactly, but this meeting does involve you. I thought you might want to be there for it."

The tension that had left my own shoulders now found its way into hers, her chin tipping up in that way I recognized as her reacting to a challenge. "What do you mean it involves me? What is this meeting? If it has to do with me, why didn't you tell me about it earlier?"

I sighed. That was a good question, and the easy answer was that I'd known it was coming but had spent all weekend enjoying her company too much to bring it up. The ice cream date had extended into an all-out movie marathon over the weekend, Olivia and I agreeing to shut the real world out completely in favor of every fictional world we could find, and I hadn't wanted to ruin any of it by telling her there was an investor meeting this morning and the subject was the way I'd hired Olivia herself.

"It's sort of last-minute," I told her, almost honestly.

I mean, I'd only known about it since Thursday night. So it was at least a little bit unexpected.

She stood and walked around her desk, her eyes hesitant. "So who are we meeting? And what exactly are we going to be talking about?"

I gave her a grin of relief at her willingness to be involved and then turned and led her out of her office and toward the boardroom.

"We're meeting the entire board. Because they want to talk about you, your credentials or lack thereof, and the fact that they think we're dating."

To her credit, she didn't even miss a stride. Instead, she lengthened her strides to catch up to me, her chin tilted and her shoulders straight.

"Right," she breathed. "So we're going to stand up in front of the firing squad and tell them why they don't actually need to shoot us. No problem."

Another bit of tension melted, though not all of it.

This meeting wasn't going to be a fun one. But I felt a whole lot better about our chances now that she was going into it with me. The girl didn't seem to have ever found a fight she couldn't win.

I was counting on that attitude to help me talk the investors into letting her stay. Because at this point, she was running the accounting department so well that I wasn't sure I could find anyone to replace her.

And I didn't really want to.

• • ⚜ • •

ED BURNS DROPPED HIS chin and looked over his glasses at Olivia in what I'd come to think of as his disappointed schoolteacher look, and when he spoke, his voice was condescending and incredibly arrogant.

He sounded like he was talking to a naughty third grader. Despite the fact that Olivia was very obviously a fully formed and very capable woman.

"You mean to tell me, young lady, that you didn't graduate at all?"

She gave him a slight smile and an even slighter shrug, like they were discussing something as inconsequential as what sort of lipstick she was wearing today. "Honestly—Mr. Burns, is it? It seemed like such a colossal waste of time when the classes were easy enough that I could have slept through them. I decided—and my counselor agreed with me—that it would be better for me to get out into the real world and get some actual experience, rather than being shut up in a classroom and bored out of my mind."

He harrumphed like this was the most ridiculous thing he'd ever heard—which really did go well with the disapproving schoolteacher metaphor I had going in my head. "Bored? You were at NYU, and you're claiming you were *bored*?"

"I'm not claiming it, Ed. I'm saying it straight out. Haven't you ever been in a class where you already knew exactly what the professor was going to say next and how to handle it? Where you could do the homework with your eyes closed and most of your brain shut off, and where you were so bored out of your mind that you were having trouble remembering why you were paying thousands of dollars to subject yourself to this torture? Surely with your keen intellect, you experienced this quite a bit. Probably even more than me."

She shut her mouth primly while I fought down the laughter I could feel building in my chest.

The woman was a freaking force of nature. I'd brought her into a meeting where the investors—or at least one of them—was intent on embarrassing her, and instead, she was showing him up so cleanly that I was surprised he still had any hair left on his head.

Of course, he didn't seem to realize how badly she was embarrassing him. But judging from the slight smiles on several other faces, the rest of the investors were noticing.

Adams, one of the other investors, evidently decided he'd seen enough and stepped in at that point. "Ed, the thing is, with or without a degree, she's improving the efficiency of the place. Literally making money for the company. That's awfully hard to argue with."

Ed Burns turned to Adams with a glare that said he didn't like being interrupted when he was torturing someone, and would have said something except another of the investors—Abramson, this time—cut in.

"I have to agree, actually," he muttered. "If she's improving the accounting department, I can't see why we'd want to get rid of her."

"Get rid of me?" Olivia asked quickly. "Oh, is that what we're here to decide on? Sorry, gentlemen—and lady," she added, with a nod to Sonya Gregory, the only other woman in the room. "I didn't realize we were deciding on my future with the company."

"Yes, well," Burns growled, "we don't like the optics of it. Leo here hired you without running it by us and without asking anyone's advice. Didn't even do a proper background check on you, from what I've heard. It doesn't look good that he had an opening and immediately inserted his newest girlfriend."

I saw the color drain from Olivia's face, but I was already turning on Ed, furious. "First, Ed, she's not my girlfriend. Second, it was a position of immediate need. We can't get by without a fully functioning accounting department, as I'm sure you realize. When Jonathan told me he was leaving, he gave me only a couple of weeks. I needed someone immediately. Or would you rather I have shut down the accounting department entirely?"

I took a breath, wondering if he was going to respond, and when he didn't, I stood and walked to the front of the room so that all eyes were on me. "I also don't particularly appreciate the implication that I hired someone I was sleeping with."

"Didn't you?" snapped Ed. "You happened to have this woman living in your house, and I'm to believe that you weren't doing anything with her? She just happened to be available, and happened to be an accountant, and you just—"

Right, that was enough of that. I slammed my hands down on the table and leaned toward him, feeling my face settle into a furious mask. "So you think I what? Went out and found a girl who was a genius with numbers, just on the off chance that I might need someone like her? And what exactly, Ed, do you think my play is here?"

"Sure is helpful to you to have the head of the accounting department in your pocket, isn't it? Or in your pants, as the case may be?"

For a moment, I was so shocked at what he'd said that my voice failed me.

I found it again quickly, though.

"That," I hissed, "is so far out of line that I'm not even sure we're still standing in the same room. The girl is a genius, Ed, and I'm not sure how you can argue with having someone so capable in charge of the money. She and I are not involved the way you evidently believe we are, and even if we were, it would be absolutely none of your business. Now, I suggest you get out. As CEO and majority stakeholder here, I have the final call on who sits on this board. I'm making an executive decision to cut you out."

Ed, true to form, started spluttering at that, horrified and shocked that I'd do something like that. "You can't do that! The contract I signed—"

"Said very clearly that I held the highest stake in the company and that I would maintain final authority over who sat on my board," I ground out. "You've just lost that privilege, Ed. Get out. My lawyers will send you paperwork to sever the business ties this afternoon."

He opened and closed his mouth like some sort of gasping fish, his eyes bulging and his face growing redder and redder, and for a moment, I thought he might actually have a stroke—or a heart attack—right there in my boardroom. Then he managed to get a hold of himself and straightened up.

"Just as well," he answered coldly. "I'm not sure I want to be involved in a company where the morals are so lax, to start with."

He turned and walked out, looking for all the world like he'd chosen to do it of his own accord.

Of course, everyone in the room knew better.

The moment the door closed behind him, I turned to the rest of the board. "I'm sorry you had to see that," I said quietly. "But I'm not sure I want someone who is obviously opposed to making money on the board of this company. He obviously doesn't have our best interests in mind."

Sonya Gregory snorted. "Honestly, I've been hoping you'd do that for months now. The man has always had a stick up his ass, and he hates women who have power. You should have heard some of the conversations I've had with him about my own position here."

I gave her a glimmer of a smile. "You should have told me sooner."

Then I turned to Olivia, expecting to see triumph or even amusement on her face at her victory here.

Instead, I saw her biting her lip and watching the door, her face transparent in her moment of inattention. And I didn't see triumph or amusement there.

I saw consideration. Doubt. Vulnerability.

And if I'd been able to read her mind, I was almost positive I would have heard her thinking that he might be right—and that she might need to leave after all.

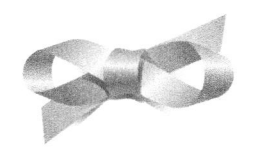

CHAPTER 11

OLIVIA

I WENT TO LUNCH IMMEDIATELY after the meeting I'd been forced to attend, and it wasn't because I was hungry. I'd had breakfast two hours ago, and I never ate when I was upset, so it wasn't like I had a sudden craving for a hamburger or anything like that.

A beer, maybe. A margarita, definitely. And with that in mind, instead of heading to a place that served food, I headed to a place where I could get a drink. With a basket of chips and salsa to go along with it.

I didn't exactly want to go back to the office drunk. Or rather... Well, I sort of did, given how my morning had been going so far. But I didn't really think that was a good idea. Things were already too sketchy when it came to me working there. The last thing I needed to do was get back into the office sloppy drunk and start making a scene.

Of course, it wasn't like I was going to be staying that much longer, anyhow. I mean, possibly not. Yes, I'd given it another week, and I meant to hold to that. But with the way things were going, I didn't know if I was going to make it much longer. Crap, even staying another week sounded like a chore.

I was also starting to worry that staying—no matter how much I wanted to—would cause real damage to Leo. I mean, I'd already known that. Of course. Roger might find me at any moment, or he might find Leo. He might figure out that Leo was helping me hide and that Leo was the only reason I had a roof over my head.

He might come after both of us.

But now, with this meeting with the investors, I'd seen a whole other danger. One that had less to do with Leo himself and more to do with his company.

He was losing investors because of me, and though he was acting as though it didn't matter, and like he'd be just fine without them—and had maybe even thought about getting rid of them on his own—I knew it couldn't be that simple. Yes, Folley was incredibly successful and wealthy. Yes, they owned many smaller companies and seemed, from what I'd seen in the accounts, to be doing just fine.

That didn't mean they could afford to throw investors to the curb like Leo was currently doing.

The thing that made me feel even worse was that he was doing it for me. His company was being punished because of his relationship with me when we didn't even have a relationship! And when I hadn't even wanted the job at all!

I picked up the margarita—on the rocks, and with plenty of salt, the way my best friend in college had taught me to drink them—and drank half of it in one gulp. Then I held my head, gasping, as the brain freeze took over.

Unfortunately, the brain freeze didn't do one single thing to help my brain figure out how to get out of this mess.

I hadn't wanted to work for Leo. I'd done it for him as a favor and nothing else. Sure, I was good at the job and helping his company become more efficient, but that had never meant I wanted to stay longer than absolutely necessary.

Especially if staying meant causing him as much trouble as I seemed to be causing him.

Brain unfrozen now, I reached for a chip and dipped it into the salsa, making a face when the chip came back barely coated in red sauce. One couldn't exactly find quality Mexican food in Minneapolis, and though I knew that New York didn't exactly deal in authentic Mexican food, either, I knew good salsa when I saw it.

This wasn't it.

Still, when I stuck it in my mouth, it did the job, setting my tongue alight with spices and taking my mind off my current troubles for at least a moment.

Only a moment, though, and then my mind turned back to a very, very big question: What was I going to do? What was my next move? Did I actually want to stay so badly that I was willing to put Leo's company at risk to do it?

And if I did, what was I hoping to get out of the deal?

Not enough, I realized. I might enjoy working in the office and getting some use out of my brain and my education, and the idea of going back to a world where I wasn't using said brain or said education might seem incredibly, horribly unfair. I might have a physical craving, an ache in my stomach, for the day-to-day interaction with the people in the office, none of whom wanted to kill me—at least, as far as I knew.

That didn't mean I had the right to endanger Leo's company or well-being.

I stuck another chip in my mouth and chewed, then finished the first margarita in one more sip and called for another.

Yes, I'd wanted to keep working with Leo for as long as I managed to stay in Minneapolis. But I wasn't willing to risk his company for that.

And that right there was the only answer I really needed.

. . ⚜ . .

I WALKED INTO HIS OFFICE the moment I got back in the building, my blood still buzzing a bit with the two margaritas I'd had to drink, my mind crystal clear when it came to knowing what I had to do.

I'd gone to lunch early to try to figure out how I was going to handle the situation with his investors—and to get away from Leo himself, as I'd known he'd almost inevitably want to talk to me about what had happened.

And now I was back to talk to him. Only I didn't think he was going to like what I had to say.

I marched in without knocking—which I assumed I could do, given that the door was open—and gave him an only slightly buzzed stare.

He, in return, looked at me like I'd lost my mind. "Hey," he said slowly. "Everything... okay?"

"No," I told him bluntly. "It's definitely not. In case you haven't noticed, I'm not too popular with your investors. In fact, I just lost you one of them."

He shrugged like it mattered less than the carpet we were currently standing on. "Who, Burns? I'm not worried about him. You heard the other investors. He didn't really fit in here, anyhow."

"But I bet his money did," I said. "Leo, I can't keep working here if I'm going to be losing you your investors, and you know it. I can't stay here if it's going to mean you putting your company in jeopardy."

He immediately stopped looking like this was all some sort of joke. "What?"

"You heard me. I can't keep working here if it's going to be a problem. I refuse to hurt your company."

"You're not hurting my company."

"And yet I just watched a rather large investor walk out of a board meeting with plans to pull his money from you," I noted. "That doesn't seem like it's *good* for the company, does it? I think you'd better consider this my notice that I'm quitting."

His face turned... stubborn. "You can't. I won't let you."

I could feel my own face matching his now. Because he couldn't just tell me that I wasn't allowed to do something.

"Actually, I can. We didn't have any contract that said I have to keep working for you. Honestly, our contract—which is just oral, by the way, not written—just said I was going to play arm candy for you. Not that I was going to be required to play accountant, too."

And now he started to look panicky. "You can't leave. I need you to stay and head up that department. It'll fall apart without leadership."

"You mean like the entire company will fall apart without investors?" I answered quickly, counting on him to see the problem there.

Unfortunately, it seemed he was a whole lot more stubborn than I'd given him credit for.

"Olivia, I don't know if you've noticed or not, but I've got quite a lot of money myself. I can very easily cover the cost of losing Ed Burns."

"And what about when other investors follow?" I asked, having already known that he'd probably pull that reasoning. "What about when other investors decide that Burns was right and that they also want out? Folley is publicly traded, right? So what happens when people out there realize that you're losing investors and start to get nervous? What if they start selling your stocks and send the company's books right into the ground? What will happen then, huh? All because you insist on keeping me in your accounting department? Is it really worth it, Leo?"

"Yes," he muttered. "If you're going to keep making changes like the ones you're making, and improving things the way you've been doing, then yes, it's worth it. Because you'll improve our efficiency, and the things you're worrying about aren't going to happen."

"I'm not so sure," I murmured. "And I'm not sure I want to risk it. I'm going to have to think about this, Leo. I'm going home early today."

I turned and left his office without waiting for an answer. And I didn't care if he was currently my boss. If he wanted to keep me, he wouldn't say one damn thing about me wanting to go home and think about whether I wanted to stay or not.

. . ∽∘∾ . .

I STOPPED ON THE WAY home at the first pay phone I saw, parked the car, jumped out, and slammed my way into the booth. A quick set of finger movements and I'd dialed Alice's number and put in the code to bill the call to the company credit card Leo had told me I could use.

And then I gave myself a moment to grin at the amount of secrecy I'd just employed in the space of five minutes. Pay phone, which was untraceable. Company credit card, which was totally not attached to my name.

Hell, I was even using a different phone than I usually went to. So if anyone was for any reason watching the phone booth I'd used in the past, they'd have no idea that I made this call at all.

It was perfect. Or rather, it would have been if I hadn't been calling her to tell her that I was probably going to be moving on again and that I didn't know when I'd be landing—and hence when I'd be available for phone calls once more.

The problem with calling Alice was, of course, that I didn't get to say much.

"My goodness, what are you doing waiting so long between phone calls?" she gasped the minute she heard my voice. "Do you know how worried I've been? I haven't heard from you in so long I thought something might have happened!"

I frowned and tried to remember how long it had been since I last called her. Then I remembered that I'd called her right after Sandy and I had gone shopping, specifically to tell her how much I'd just spent on a single dress. She'd been both amused and horrified.

And that meant I'd spoken to her on Friday. It was only Monday.

"You didn't hear from me for two days," I noted calmly. "That doesn't seem like a good reason for calling out the guard, Al."

She huffed, though I could tell her heart wasn't really in it. "That's easy for you to say. Your best friend isn't being hunted down by some psycho alcoholic who may or may not have ties to the mob."

I pressed my lips together at that, mostly because I didn't have an answer for her.

Did I really think Roger had ties to the mob? Did I actually think he could throw any weight around when it came to coming after me?

The problem was, I didn't have a good answer for that. And as long as I didn't know for a fact that he *didn't* have ties to the mob, it was a whole lot safer to assume that he did and to act accordingly.

"Point taken," I said, appropriately apologetic. "Would it make you feel better if I called you once a day?"

"Yes," she said primly. "Now, what's up? Or did you call to do more gloating about how much you're spending in the city?"

I hadn't. This time, I wasn't gloating at all. I went quickly through the corporate dinner, which I hadn't updated her on, and the meeting we'd just had with the investors, and ended with the idea that I didn't think I could stay any longer. I was causing too much trouble in Leo's life.

"I might actually cost him his company, if he's not careful," I finished.

She didn't even take a second to think about it. "Olivia, do you think he's gotten to where he is by being a bad businessman?"

"No," I said, confused. What did that have to do with anything?

"And do you think he doesn't know how to deal with investors? Or the real world?"

My frown deepened. "No."

"Then why in heaven's name are you trying to second-guess him when it comes to how he runs his company and deals with his own investors?"

"Well, when you put it that way—"

"I do put it that way. You're in a safe place and doing something you really seem to be enjoying, and don't even get me started on how much happier you seem now that you're with Leo. The work suits you. The company suits you. I bet that overly expensive dress even suits you. Stop trying to find a reason to leave."

"But what if—"

"Do you think Roger can get to you there?"

That brought me up short. I was terrified that he'd find me, but even if he figured out where I was... Did I actually believe he'd be able to get through Leo and get to me?

Did I really?

"No," I breathed. "Leo makes me feel safe."

"Then stop trying to find a reason to leave him. Stay put until and unless you have a better offer. Got it? Don't make me come all the way to the city and handcuff you to his bedpost just to make sure you're out of harm's way. Because I'll do it. You know I will."

I didn't answer her.

Mostly because I was wondering whether she knew that I'd slept with him...

Or that handcuffing me to his bedpost didn't sound like the worst way to keep me in his apartment and safe from Roger.

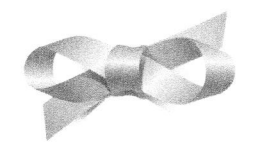

CHAPTER 12

LEO

"MR. FOLLEY, YOU HAVE a call on the line, but I'm not completely sure you'll want to take it," my assistant's voice said, sounding tinny and fake through the intercom system that connected her desk to mine.

I frowned. If she didn't think I'd want to take a call, she usually sent it right through to voicemail or took a message. She didn't call me—while the person I might not want to talk to was presumably on the line—and tell me that I might not want to talk to said person.

"So..." I led. "Are you going to tell me anything more than that, or are you just planning to make me guess who the person might be based on the idea that I may or may not want to talk to them?"

My assistant didn't smile. But I swear, when she spoke again, she sounded lighter, somehow. Like she might actually be considering it. "Not a guessing game, sir. I don't have time for that, and I suspect you don't, either. The caller is Mark Parker. Again. I'm quite happy to tell him that you're currently busy in the archery studio below the building, if you like, but if you want to talk to him..."

"Janice, did you just make a joke?" I asked, shocked as all get out.

The girl was good, but no one around here knew her for her sense of humor. I didn't think I'd ever even heard her laugh before.

"If you want to call it that," she replied primly. "Do you want me to get rid of him, or do you want to talk to him?"

I bit my lip and turned to stare through the window of my office. Now that she'd presented it that way, I actually appreciated that she'd given me the option. Mark Parker was a big shot with offices in at least ten different cities—and that was only in the US. He didn't specialize in any one thing, or at least he didn't anymore, but rather owned a company that operated a lot like Folley, with many, many departments and branches.

Only they were about fifty times as big as my little place.

A quick search of my knowledge banks reminded me, too, that Parker's company had grown a whole lot faster than people had thought possible. It had been a startup one day and a multibillion-dollar company later in the same month, gobbling up smaller companies so fast that more than one person had assumed that Parker himself had millions in the bank and was funding everything on his own rather than counting on traditional business practices like loans.

Personally, I'd always thought that the guy had taken out loans but that those loans hadn't come from traditional institutions like banks. No, if I'd been a betting man, I'd have put very good money down on him having gotten his funding right from the New York mob.

Yeah, yeah, make fun of me if you must, but the guy had that feel about him. The greasy, slicked-back hair. The too-large chin. The booming voice that somehow made you feel like you were being forced up against the wall just through the sheer noise of it.

Yes, I'd talked to him before. And yes, if he was calling me today, I was pretty sure I knew exactly what he was calling about.

"I'll talk to him," I told Janice, taking grim pleasure in the idea that I was going to be able to tell the blustering bully once again that I had no intention of letting Folley fall into the bottomless pit that was Parker Products.

I sat through the multiple clicks that said Janice was transferring a call, straightening my shoulders and injecting even more steel into my spine. Contact with Mark Parker was never easy. He was larger than life and thought that everyone should do exactly what he wanted them to.

Unfortunately for him, I wasn't the kind of guy he could push around.

"Folley, how are you?" the familiar too-friendly voice boomed over the phone.

I held the phone away from my ear until he finished talking, wishing I had a way to turn down the volume, and smirked. "Parker, you must be a glutton for punishment. Aren't you tired of hearing me tell you no yet?"

Now the friendliness dropped right out of his voice, the way it always did when he didn't get the answer he wanted. "Folley, don't be a fool. I'm offering you a better deal than anyone else will ever offer you. Ten billion, with half of it up front and the rest payable in a year, once I see what you've got. And you'll get to stay on at the company. Play top dog for as long as you want. Keep your own office and everything."

I closed my eyes and shook my head. Yes, the offer had gone up. He was offering twice as much as he had been last year.

That still didn't mean I was going to take it.

"It would be a great deal," I agreed. "But the company's still not for sale. And even if it was, I would never agree to work for you. I'm pretty sure we've been over this multiple times. I like owning the company. I like the size of the thing. I don't plan on selling out, and I definitely don't plan on answering to anyone else."

"Do you plan to get a new investor in to replace Burns?" he asked bluntly. "Because I know how much money he had in your company. I know how much it's going to hurt your bottom line to lose him."

I didn't even miss a beat. Yes, that had just happened this morning, and I was a bit surprised that word had traveled so quickly, but I also wouldn't have put it past Mark Parker to have spies in my company or even on my board. Still, it would do me any good to let him know I suspected as much.

"Did you also know that I was the one who invited *him* to leave?" I asked, feeling more than a little bit cocky. "Did you hear about me actually kicking him off my board and making the arrangements to buy his stock myself?"

The deep, surprised silence on the other end of the line told me that he had not, in fact, known about that.

"I'll take that as a no," I said, unable to keep the grin off my face. "And as long as I'm giving you information you didn't have before, I'll give you a bit more. I hadn't been planning on kicking him out, but it turns out it worked well for me. I went from owning 51 percent of the company to owning 73 percent. And you know what that makes me? Even steadier in my position."

"Even more dependent on the company doing well," he retorted immediately. "Even more fucked if it turns out that stock keeps dropping like it is."

"It won't," I replied. "It's dropping right now because people are worried about me cutting down on my board. But I've been with this company from the start. I know how to make it successful. And after our numbers rise even higher this quarter, the stock will go through the roof."

I couldn't see Parker, obviously, but I could just imagine his face frowning darker and darker with every sentence I uttered.

And it might have been horrible, but I was loving every second of it. I loved being the one to give him bad news. The man was a bully and a crook, and as far as I was concerned, anything that took him down a rung or two was worthwhile.

"What makes you so sure you'll recover?" he growled.

I noted that he was no longer trying to be my friend and felt a whole lot better in this new position.

"New head of accounting," I said. "And she's fucking brilliant. Already increasing our bottom line. Improving our efficiencies. She's going to revolutionize the company, and she's only been here a week. So even if Folley doesn't buy anything else this quarter, our numbers will look better in two months than they do right now."

"I doubt it," he said, as if he knew something I didn't. "If she's that good, someone's going to come in and steal her from you, and then you'll come crawling back to me begging you for the deal."

"Doubtful," I shot back. "But you can call me again in six months and see how I feel about it then."

I hung up without waiting for a reply, loving even more that he was never going to see that coming, and sat back in my chair.

I hadn't been lying when I told him that Olivia was revolutionizing the company.

I just didn't know if she'd be willing to keep doing it... or if she was going to follow through on her threat to quit.

And if Parker was sniffing around the company again, it just got a whole lot more important for me to keep her on board.

. . ⚜ . .

I GOT HOME, MY HEART somewhere in the vicinity of my throat as I hit the button to open the elevator and crept through the rooms it took to get from there to the kitchen.

This area of the house had never been that important to me before, but since Olivia arrived, it had somehow become central to my life. We did a lot of our talking in the kitchen, hanging over the counter, and almost all of our eating at the small table in the breakfast nook. This was where we'd discussed business and the contract we had together, and where she'd told me a little bit more about her own thoughts on some of the books I had in my library.

It was where she'd modeled some of the clothes she'd bought during that first shopping trip. It was where I'd kissed her, unable to stop myself.

I walked into the opening right before the kitchen, my breath catching in my throat and my steps light and hesitant at the thought that I might walk into the kitchen to find it completely deserted. Because when I left this morning, Olivia had still had things spread all across the counter. The place had definitely looked like it belonged at least half to her.

If she'd decided she was going to quit Folley—and me—I was guessing the kitchen would be sparkling clean and devoid of any of her possessions. Hell, if she'd decided to leave, it wouldn't have surprised me to walk into the apartment and found that she was already gone, her mind made up and her eyes firmly on her next destination.

When I saw the makeup bag on the counter, I thought that was exactly what she was doing. Gathering whatever she'd left in the kitchen and packing it away. A quick glance and I also saw another bag on the chair, this one a sort of backpack that looked full.

Oh shit, I thought, my stomach sinking. She *was* packing. She was doing that thing you do when you take a bag around the house for one final pass, to make sure you haven't missed anything.

She was leaving. And she wasn't even going to tell me about it. She was just going to up and run, like a thief in the night.

And she was going to take a very large piece of me with her.

When I finally came to her sitting at the kitchen table, in a terry cloth robe rather than traveling clothes, I was so relieved that I actually started laughing.

She looked up, her eyes big and her hands going immediately to her hair—which looked wet and wild, like she'd just come out of the bath.

"What are you laughing at?" she gasped. "Do I have something on my face?"

I shook my head, walked toward her, and leaned down to place a soft, sweet kiss on her forehead. "I'm just happy to see you here," I breathed. "I thought for sure that you'd be gone."

She gave me a very wry, very sarcastic look. "Leo, I may be a lot of things. But I would never run from someone I cared about without saying goodbye first."

A shadow crossed her face at her words, like she actually had done just that in the past, but she put it away very quickly, and I was too hung up on the words she'd used to think too much about it—or the kiss I'd just given her.

"I'm just glad to see you," I repeated. "Do you want to get dinner?"

"Yes," she replied immediately. "I'm starved. And tonight, movies. And no talk about work. I want my brain to have a night off from thinking about the office and what I'm going to do. Deal?"

I agreed to it immediately. Yes, I wanted to know what she was going to do, and I was dying to talk to her about the offer from Parker.

But after having come home positive that I'd find her gone, the option of having a night alone with her—without the office taking up any of her attention—sounded like it just might be heaven itself. And after the day I'd had, I could use a little bit of heaven in my life.

CHAPTER 13

OLIVIA

"GIRL, I JUST HEARD a bunch of investors might pull out of the company just because you're fucking Leo."

I almost dropped the coffeepot—and the mug I was filling—in shock. Not only at the sudden incursion into my coffee break, but at the words themselves.

"Excuse me?" I snapped, half-horrified and half-furious.

I spun around, ready to heave the coffeepot in question at whoever would dare to come in here and use that sort of language but stopped myself just in time because it was just Sandy.

"Sandy," I hissed. "Do you know how close I just came to hurling this coffee pot at you? Watch your mouth!"

She smirked. "Well, for what it's worth, I think they're insane. You obviously know exactly what you're doing. You're the best supervisor the accounting department has ever had, if you ask me."

I gave her the best side-eye I could manage on such short notice. "You work in sales. How would you know what makes a good supervisor in accounting?"

She leaned in, her voice dropping. "You're the only one who's ever caught on to Bradley Stephens cheating on his expense account, and as far as I'm concerned, that makes you the best supervisor they've ever had in that department."

I tried to keep my face serious. Honestly, I did.

But it was really, really hard to do that when Sandy, the biggest gossip in the entire company, as far as I knew, was whispering to me what she obviously considered to be a really juicy secret. True, it was a secret that had to do with one of the sales guys stealing money from the company, so it wasn't really a laughing matter, but still.

There was something about Sandy passing along news like that, with her wide eyes and pursed mouth, that made it impossible to get mad at her.

"To be fair," I told her frankly, "I probably only saw it because I was new and going through everything, trying to learn names and positions and who did what and where. For all you know, it could have just been a fluke."

It wasn't. But I wasn't going to tell her that. I also wasn't going to tell her that Bradley wasn't the only employee I'd found cheating on his numbers—or that I'd recommended that every employee who was doing it be written up and put under better supervision, to try to keep them from doing it again in the future.

It was a whole lot more fun for Sandy—and therefore, the rest of the office—to think I'd found it by luck. Better for them not to think that I was actively looking at all of them to see whether they were doing the same thing.

Better, all told, for them to think I didn't really know what I was doing, and that I'd just gotten lucky. That way they wouldn't think about how to hide any of their other actions from me.

Yeah, yeah, that sort of defeated the purpose of me being a supervisor, and it definitely didn't do much for the rumor that Leo had hired someone who wasn't qualified for the job, but I'd always found it really convenient for people to underestimate me. Play the airhead convincingly enough and they'll never see your intelligence. Which means they'll never see you coming.

Unfortunately, sometimes that makes them mad. Like when Roger suddenly realized that I wasn't going to stand for him beating up my mom anymore.

Aaaaand back to the issue with the office, I told myself firmly. Roger wasn't my problem right now. Deciding whether I was going to stay here was.

"So you don't think the entire board should quit just because Leo hired me?" I asked, trying to look like I needed encouragement and moral support.

Sandy blew a raspberry at the idea that the board might even know what they were talking about. "They might quit. But they'd be idiots to do it. I've heard more than one exec talking about how much you've improved everything in the department, and the board would be smart to look at that sort of thing. Besides, if they think Leo's actually going to fire you, they've got another think coming."

Okay, I hadn't been expecting her to go *there*.

"What does that mean?" I asked, truly confused.

She gave me a very coy smile. "Well, you can't see it because your back is usually turned, but whenever you walk away from him, he looks at you like you're the greatest gift to man. Or greatest gift to him, anyhow. You're not just some floozy he hired because he was dating you. You've got all the goods. And he knows it."

My stomach did an entire flip inside my body, and a second later, all of my other organs started dancing, too.

What. The. Heck?

Leo watched me when I walked away from him? Looking like he thought I was the world's greatest gift to man?

Was that before or after his board had started quitting because of me?

"Um, thank you?" I said, not really sure how to respond to this new bit of news.

Luckily, Sandy had already moved on to something else. She waved away my thanks and got even closer to me, completely ignoring the hot coffeepot I was still holding.

"And that's not the half of it," she whispered, her face taking on the glow of someone who's about to pass on news that she definitely shouldn't be passing on. "It's not like you're the only ones who are dating around here."

I narrowed my eyes and tipped my head, inviting her to go on.

Were there other execs who were hooking up? And if there were...

"Gerald from HR and Shawna from IT," she hissed, sounding like this was the most exciting thing that had ever happened. "I just caught them making out in the supply cabinet!"

My heart fell. Okay, not execs, then. And if they were just HR and IT... then not people I could really use to support my own position. No one was going to care if people like that were dating.

I would just look stupid if I told anyone it was okay for Leo and me to be dating if people like Gerald and Shawna could do it.

Not that I was going to tell anyone anything like that. I didn't think it was okay for Leo and me to be dating. Or rather... Well, I wasn't sure I had any problem with Leo and me dating, and I damn well wasn't sure that I wanted to stop dating him. If that was even what we were doing.

But I wasn't going to stick around in the office if it meant that I was putting his company—and his well-being—at risk. It wasn't worth it. Yes, I loved the job. Yes, I loved using my brain, and for someone that I actually really liked.

But when my presence might actually be a detriment? That was a hard no.

I muttered something to Sandy about how she should probably turn them in for making out on company property at the very least, and then made my way back to my desk, my mind one step closer to made up about leaving this company and letting Folley fend for itself without me.

CHAPTER 14

OLIVIA

THE PROBLEM WITH DECIDING to quit, of course, was that I had to go into Leo's office and tell him—again—that I was finished with this game. And I didn't have any doubt that I'd be facing the same exact arguments from him, and I also didn't doubt that they'd be just as good this time as they had been last time.

But I knew in my heart that I was doing the right thing. I didn't make friends easily, and I definitely didn't fall for guys often, so the fact that I'd not only come in here and started feeling at home but had also started having real feelings for Leo meant that this was a whole new world for me.

I flat-out wasn't willing to mess the biggest piece of that world up just because I wanted to be prideful and keep working here. Sure, I still had another week on the oral agreement we'd done, to include the final dinner that he wanted me to help him with, but that didn't mean I actually had to be in the office making trouble for him. And eventually, he'd come to see that I was right about that.

I walked right to my desk, thinking that this would all be easier if I found a way to do it without actually having to face him, and started going through my drawers. The thing was, I hadn't been in the office that long, and I'd gone out of my way not to bring anything personal because it might have given someone insight into who I actually was—or given someone else a way to identify me to anyone who was calling around looking for me.

Yeah, I sounded paranoid as hell to even be thinking that sort of thing, but what would you have done in my situation? Honestly?

Pens, pens, pens, and a pen holder that had come with the desk. Right. I slid the first drawer closed, knowing that all of that could—and should—stay here, and went into the next one. This one contained all of the files I'd built on every employee in the time I'd been here, as well as the notes I'd made on the company's systems and how they could all be improved.

My hand paused over those because they were mine. That was my hard work sitting in that drawer right there. My brainpower down on paper and my ideas set down in pen—in my writing.

Then I realized two things: 1. Roger didn't know what my writing looked like, so it wouldn't matter if he could see it. Hell, I didn't even know if the jerk could read. So that wasn't a problem at all. And 2. Those notes would all come in handy for whoever replaced me.

My heart quaked a little bit at that last bit, and the thought that someone else would be sitting in this desk in a couple of days, going through the information I'd collected, maybe grabbing the phone and calling Leo up for a quick meeting about something that had originally been my idea...

But I put the jealousy and the feel of my heart cracking down the center to the side. It wasn't my place to think about stuff like that. Leo wasn't anything to me, and I wasn't doing myself or him any favors by thinking this could be more than it was. I was just a girl who had been in the right place at the right time and had agreed to help him. That was all. I'd done what I'd promised I would do, and I'd stay for the next five days to finish out my agreement with him.

Then I would hit the road again, because that was the best and safest thing for everyone.

And if I was going to end up leaving a piece of my heart—and that wonderful apartment, and all that hot water, and those books—behind me when I left?

I forced a shrug, allowed myself one sigh, and closed the drawer. So what if I was leaving a piece of myself behind? It wasn't the first time I'd done it, and I'd survived before. I'd survive again.

Seriously.

At that moment, a hand fell on my shoulder, making me jump out of my chair and whirl around, heart racing and the sound of my pulse pounding in my ears.

Of course, when I turned around, I saw that it was only Sandy. Again.

"Woman, if you keep sneaking up on me like that, you're going to get a stapler thrown at your head. Or worse," I muttered, slumping back into my seat.

She grinned, showing that she definitely wasn't sorry for having snuck up on me, but the smile died away when she took in the still-empty box on my desk. "What are you doing? Moving offices?" she asked, frowning.

"Nope. Leaving," I said shortly. "The board is right. It's not a good idea for me to stay, and I'm just going to end up hurting Leo if I do. I'm going to ruin his reputation and force all the investors to leave. Kill the company."

"But you're so good at your job," Sandy argued. "You can't be good at your job and kill the company at the same time."

I reached out, snagged a pad of paper that I knew for a fact actually was mine, and popped it into the box, my eyes on Sandy's. "They'll find someone else who's good at this job," I assured her. "And no one in their right mind will care that they're the ones running the accounting department rather than me."

Her frown just deepened. "And what about Leo? What about dating him?"

I blew out another breath. "We're not actually dating, you know. It's nothing that serious. He'll be better off without me, too."

She drew back, shocked. "Wait, you're talking about leaving entirely? Like... not just leaving the office?"

I shoved my purse into the box, thinking that I didn't have anything else in the desk that was actually mine, and started to get up. "That's right. His reputation will be better without me here. *He'll* do better without me here."

Sandy's face went from shocked to stubborn, though, and she reached out and shoved me right back into my seat, then whirled my seat around so it was facing my computer again. "Girl, you obviously don't read the paper, if that's what you think. Look."

Before I could respond to that and tell her that I had a whole lot more on my plate than just reading the paper, she was leaning over me and pulling up Google on my computer. A quick search on Leo's name brought up page after page of hits, and though I was surprised at how many there were—how many articles could there be about one insanely handsome billionaire businessman, after all?—I was more surprised at the titles.

Leo Folley Finally Finds Love! one read, making me snort. Love? That was far-fetched.

Is the Biggest Playboy in Town Finally Settling Down? the next asked. That got another huff from me... but the line underneath caught my attention. *Leo Folley, the billionaire that we've all been cheering for since he was a kid, might have finally found his match, and we couldn't be happier.*

Wait.

Sandy scrolled through article after article, and before long, I started to see a theme. They weren't making fun of him for dating me. They were... happy for him. The press was actually raving—and not only about Leo. Soon there were articles about me, that called out how well

I was doing at the company and how insiders were saying that I might just increase Folley's numbers for the next quarter.

They were calling me brainy. Saying I was better with numbers than anyone Folley had ever had before. And they were saying that I'd had a good influence on Leo himself, who had started going to parties and charity events and giving money at every one of them.

"They think I'm... good for him?" I whispered.

"Better than that. They think you're saving him from a life of being forever an unhappy bachelor," Sandy said, also whispering. "You don't know how much this town likes that guy. Everyone has been cheering for him since he took over his dad's company, and we've all wanted to see him happy. This one office employs a ton of people, and the city itself would be the poorer if Folley went under. If you're saving the company while dating the guy, then it makes you..."

My mouth quirked. "Sort of a Wonder Woman," I said.

Sandy clicked on another article—this one more on me than on Leo—and pulled it up. "More than sort of. You're the city's hero. Though I'd suggest you start letting them get some real photos of you. They're not going to be satisfied with the back of your head for long."

I didn't answer that one. Because this whole being a heroine thing was new information to me, and yeah, I could see why the press might want better photographs of the girl they'd decided was going to save the city.

That didn't mean I could give them their wish. Because hero or not, I still didn't want anyone seeing my face or taking notice of me. It was just too dangerous.

· · ❧ · ·

I HUSTLED OUT OF THE office without saying anything to Leo, partially because I was a big fat chicken who didn't know what she wanted to say and partially because seeing all of those articles and knowing what my presence was doing for Leo's reputation...

Well, it would have been selling it short to say it muddied the waters more than a little bit.

I had never, ever thought that I might be actually helping him by playing his arm candy. Yeah, he'd said something about his publicist insisting on it, but I'd thought that was just something he was joking about. Honestly, I hadn't really thought too much about why he was paying me—in hot water and food, at the moment—to stick around. I'd just taken it at face value and gone about my life.

Weird and surreal as it had become.

I slid through the front doors, the box full of one notebook and my purse on my hip and my eyes on the ground, trying to make sense of this new information—and trying to figure out where it fit into my whole *he's better off without me* theme.

The two things didn't really seem to fit together. And I definitely wasn't sure what to do about that. I wasn't even sure there was anything to do about that. Was it an equal trade? Helping his reputation in exchange for possible putting his life at risk? Putting my life at risk—while getting to live in that apartment and enjoy all the wealth?

Putting my life at risk... while not wanting to leave the man I thought I might be falling in love with?

I shied away from that thought, my legs following the sidestep my mind had just taken, and stumbled on the curb I hadn't seen coming.

Strong, warm hands reached out to grab me, keeping me on my feet, and I looked up, laughing and about to thank whoever had saved me, when I froze.

I knew those eyes, which shifted between blue and green depending on his mood. I knew that chin. The nose. The sweep of chestnut-colored hair across the forehead.

The cocky arch of the brow as he recognized me, too.

"Mark Parker," I breathed. "What in the fucking hell are you doing here?"

His eyes narrowed, his face telling me he was just as shocked to see me as I was to see him. "Olivia. I could ask the same thing of you." His eyes swiveled from me to the building behind me and then back, and suddenly his face cleared. "You're the one they've been taking pictures of. You're his new head of accounting."

Shit. Shit, shit, shit. Of all the things I could deal with in the entire world, Mark Parker knowing where I worked—and what I was doing there, and therefore where I was sleeping, if he read the paper—was the last thing I wanted.

I couldn't have that. I *couldn't*. It would put everything at risk.

"I don't know what you're talking about," I told him coldly. "Stay away from me, or I'll call the cops."

I turned and got away from him as quickly as I could, trying very, very hard to look like I wasn't running—while at the same time demanding that my legs take the longest steps they possibly could.

Because the very last thing I wanted right now was for someone to see me on the sidewalk in front of Folley talking to Mark Parker. Or worse, recognize me and take a picture of it.

CHAPTER 15

LEO

I DRAGGED MYSELF HOME after a very long, very annoying day at the office with my head once again full of doubts. I hadn't seen Olivia—or talked to her—since the board meeting, and though I was completely fine with how that meeting had gone and the idea that Burns himself was finished having any say in my company or my life, Olivia had seemed...

Less than confident. More than that. She'd seemed like she was ready to walk out of there. She'd told me she was taking an early day to think about whether she could stay or not and walked quickly out of my office, and that had been that.

It hadn't been a fight. Hell, it hadn't even been an argument. Instead, she'd been... well, completely calm about the whole thing, like she didn't think it really mattered that much.

I didn't know if she thought I secretly wanted her to quit or if she'd just wanted to quit and had found a convenient reason. I also wasn't sure which made my heart hurt worse. All I really knew was that my heart was hurting over the whole thing, in a way that made me distinctly uncomfortable.

How had this woman become so important in my life that she was making me react like this? How had she managed to wind her way right into my everyday world, like a spider spinning a web and tangling me up in it? How had she managed to extend that reach all the way to my company and the operations there?

And what was I going to do about it if she'd decided to dismantle the entire thing?

I was also, I thought grimly as I hit the button for the penthouse in my building, getting really, really tired of going home and half expecting the place to be empty when I got there. Not that I thought she'd have cleared out today. No, she'd made it sound like she wanted to talk about the accounting job later, and leaving would definitely make that more difficult.

I was still going home to a situation where she might be getting ready to give me bad news, though, and that was hardly any better.

When the doors slid open on my foyer, I stood in the elevator for a long moment, my eyes on the hallway that led from the foyer through the library and living room to the kitchen. I couldn't see anything from here, of course, except the dim lighting of the hallway and the brighter lighting of the living room ahead of me. There were no lights on in the library, which was pretty standard, and I could see the kitchen beyond everything, where the bright white lights were glowing the way they always did.

I didn't see anyone in any of the rooms. Then again, I was seeing a very small view of all of those rooms, so it might have been insane for me to expect to see someone conveniently standing within view.

"Also, ridiculous that you're standing in the elevator staring like you're afraid of what you might see," I growled at myself. "Pathetic."

I took one stride forward, and then another, and then another, walking more quickly as I went and still lecturing myself. What the hell was I so afraid of? This was my freaking house, and it had been before I even met Olivia Cadwell—or whatever name she was using today—and it would be mine long after she left. Or didn't leave.

I was just really, really hoping it was the latter. And I wasn't used to hoping things like that.

I was used to not caring.

That, I realized, was the problem. I'd never cared whether anyone else stayed or good, and it turned out I wasn't reacting well to suddenly worrying over whether a girl was going to stay in my life or not.

I emerged from the hallway into the living room, my eyes wary, and noted quickly that there was no one in here. Not that it was a big surprise. The room basically centered around the TV, and I'd already noticed that when push came to shove, Olivia went for books over television.

I frowned and took three steps backward, my eyes going back into the library. Lights off, as I'd already known, and empty.

Maybe she was in the kitchen or her room.

Or maybe she'd already left.

I stifled the groan that brought with it and went striding into the kitchen, telling myself once again that it didn't matter if she'd left. My life would just go back to being the way it had been before she arrived.

It was a good life. It wouldn't kill me to have her gone.

Of course, the moment I walked into the kitchen, I found her sitting cross-legged on the counter, a book in her lap and her face creased into a frown of thought.

"The reading chairs not comfortable enough for you?" I joked, dropping my briefcase on the table and doing my best to walk casually toward the refrigerator, as if I hadn't been just wondering whether she was still in the apartment or not.

Olivia looked up, surprised enough at my sudden appearance to make me think she hadn't been paying attention to the real world at all. "The light is better in here than it is in the library, and my head's been hurting enough for that to be valuable. Besides, the counter isn't uncomfortable."

I snorted. "If you're small enough to fit on it, I guess. I still think the chairs would be better, myself." I swung the door of the fridge open, grabbed the bottle of rosé we'd started last night, and held it up, my eyebrows lifted in silent question.

"Oh," Olivia said, looking like the idea of having wine was also a surprise. "Yeah, sure."

I tilted my head a bit. "Why do you act like it's an earth-shattering idea to have wine? I thought the wine cupboard was your second stop anytime you came in."

She smirked. "The first being...?"

"The library, obviously," I replied with a nod to the book.

She made a wry face and set it to the side. "Honestly, I'm barely even paying attention to it. Just gave my eyes something to look at while my brain worked on some problems."

I repressed the sight that wanted to rise up from my lungs. Already going to the problems, then.

Terrific.

I mean, on one hand, yeah, terrific. It meant we'd get this out of the way right now rather than letting it fester. On the other hand...

Was it too much to ask to have a glass of wine before we dove right into the heavy stuff?

Evidently, that wasn't my call to make, though. I poured two glasses of rosé—good stuff that somehow only cost $10 a bottle—and handed one glass to Olivia, then took a sip of my own. The wine coated my tongue and slid down my throat, doing its best to give me some liquid courage in a hurry, and I took advantage of that.

"What sort of hard problems is your brain working on?"

Like I had to ask. Sandy had told me, when I cornered her and asked about a rumor I was hearing about two employees having been caught in a closet together, that Olivia had packed up her desk and left. I hadn't known Olivia had gone so far as to pack her things, but I was guessing that the action itself was what she was trying to puzzle through right now.

Another wry look from her. "The question of whether I can actually keep working at your company or not."

"Of course you can. We've already been through this. I'm the boss and I want you there, and I'm pretty sure that effectively covers you in terms of staying employed."

I was trying to make it a joke. It didn't work.

"And yet I'm not going to stay if it means burning your company to the ground," she replied seriously. "Regardless of what you as boss think. I'm not willing to do it, Leo. Period."

"Olivia, my company is not going to burn to the ground."

"You sure about that? Have you heard that a guy and girl were caught in the closet together, literally? Other people are starting to date, and you know it's because they think you and I are dating. They think that if we're dating, it's okay for them to do it."

Something about the way she said it made it quite clear that *she* didn't think we were dating. Which, I guessed, was technically true. Technically, we weren't anything to one another. We just had an agreement to look like we were dating for a set period of time.

A period of time that was almost up.

But the casual and straightforward reference to us not actually dating sent an arrow piercing right through my heart, which meant that it took me a moment to get myself together enough to answer her.

"I did hear, yes, and I already talked to them. Actually, they didn't use us as a model at all, so that should make you feel better. The male lead in that particular duo was quite clear on one point: They fell in love while they were working together. They didn't date before either of them started working at Folley. Which, according to him, made their case... better than ours."

I added that last bit hesitantly, though honestly, I thought it should have made her feel better.

Unfortunately, it seemed to do the opposite. She rolled her eyes and pursed her lips together like this was the most ridiculous thing she'd ever heard.

"And how long until more people are doing it? How long before the board hears about it and starts putting two and two together? How long until everyone else starts to pressure you about getting rid of me to restore peace and ethics in your office?"

I snorted so hard I nearly sent rosé shooting through my nose. "Peace and ethics? Is that the new goal for any corporation to shoot for?"

"Well, it should be," she said, going back to the book I knew she wasn't actually reading. "They're important qualities."

More important than love? I wondered but didn't ask.

Instead, I decided to jump to a different topic. I wasn't going to make any headway with her when it came to staying at Folley. That much was obvious. She was stubborn enough to have to make up her own mind about it, and stubborn enough that she would start disliking me for trying to alter her path.

I hadn't known her long, but I already knew that she was one of the strongest women I'd ever met. She wasn't going to let me sway her. At least... not consciously.

"Do you know Mark Parker?" I asked, trying to catch her off guard.

She looked up at me, the answer clear as day on her face, but quickly wiped it off for something more neutral. "Never heard of him. Why?"

She was lying. She knew who he was.

"I happened to look out my window this afternoon and saw you talking to him on the street below the building."

She made a show of looking like she'd just discovered something. "Oh, that guy that almost ran me over at the curb? No, I don't know him. Just some guy asking for directions."

Another lie. Which meant he'd said something important to her, and she wasn't going to tell me what it was.

I didn't like that. I liked it even less when I thought about how she'd given me the last name of Parker when she told me who she said she really was.

Yes, it was a common last name. Yes, the chances of her being related to Mark were minimal. But she was also lying to me about knowing him. Why?

I nodded like I believed her and took up my phone, hearing several emails come in at the same time. A quick scroll told me that Janice had already received several responses to the ad she'd put up for a new head of accounting. That was very fast. Some of them even looked good, according to her message. We might have Olivia replaced by the end of the week.

Though that was the last thing I wanted. I needed her in the accounting department, improving our numbers and efficiency. Especially if I was going to keep convincing the board that we needed to keep Mark Parker at arm's length.

It was ironic, when you thought about it. I needed Olivia Parker—if that was her real name—to keep Mark Parker away from my company. And now she was lying to me about whether she knew him or not.

More importantly, though, I wanted Olivia to stay for myself. Yes, the work she was doing for the company was important. But thinking about coming home to an empty house again or eating dinner without her snark and laughter on the other side of the dinner table...

I desperately wanted her to stay. I just didn't know how to make that happen—or even if she wanted to.

CHAPTER 16

OLIVIA

I WAS IN THE LIBRARY trying to decide how upset Leo would actually get if I read his rare edition of Poe when my phone rang. Or rather... when a text appeared.

I looked at the phone distrustfully, seeing that there was a text icon but not having the first clue where it had come from—or who—and grimaced. I didn't like using the thing, and I thought it made me far too easy to track, but what harm could really come from looking at a text? The other person wouldn't even be able to see that I'd read it, since I'd chosen not to share that sort of thing when I first set the phone up.

Hey, I didn't like people knowing that I'd read something and having expectations about an immediate response. Sometimes I liked to read messages and sit on them for a while before I gave anyone an answer.

"Besides," I whispered to myself. "Who could it be? Alice and Leo are the only ones who even have this number."

Leo. A chill ran over my skin at the thought of him, followed by a hot flush that I recognized as my reaction to caring way too much about someone I wasn't sure I could have. I really had to be an idiot. Falling for the guy who'd just hired me to be his date for the week and had then extended that into two weeks. A guy who had more money than I could ever dream of having—and a guy who wouldn't thank me one bit for leading my mom's psycho boyfriend to his door.

If it came to that.

The point stood, though. I really had to get my emotions under control when it came to Leo. I was way too attached to him, and that was leading me to make all sorts of stupid decisions. Or, as the case may be, failing to make decisions that I knew I needed to make.

And that had precisely nothing to do with the question of whether or not I was going to look at the text currently sitting on my phone.

I thumbed the phone on, hit the messages icon, and saw that the text had, indeed, come from Leo.

I didn't like the silly little hiccup my heart gave at the idea that he was texting me. I didn't like it at all. I also didn't like the warmth that was flooding me somewhere in my lower stomach area.

I had no right to be feeling things like that.

I hit his thread and pulled up the text, then smiled.

Leo: *We're going to my parents' city place for dinner. Hope you don't mind.*

I thought about my response for a moment, then smiled even more broadly, and started typing.

Olivia: *Is that your idea of giving me fair notice? Because it's really not. Do I have to run out and buy something for this shindig?*

Given how much he'd been insisting on me going shopping, I wouldn't have been surprised if he said yes. Sure, I'd already met his parents, but I didn't know if there was some secret Folley requirement for Dressing Up In New Clothes when we went to a city dinner rather than a family barbecue at the country house.

I mean, it sounded like a rich person thing to do. Different rules for different environments.

Leo: *No, you don't have to buy anything. Jeans and a T-shirt will do.*
Olivia: *Really? Do I even have to wear shoes?*
Leo: *I'd recommend it. Have you seen the streets? Filthy.*

I grinned outright at that... then caught myself grinning and wiped it right off my face. The man had a wicked sense of humor, true enough, and made me laugh more than almost anyone else in my entire life. That didn't mean I could get used to it or enjoy it too much.

After all, at the end of this week, I'd be moving on.

Still, the thought that he made me laugh so much brought me right to the other person who never failed to make me laugh. My mother, with her flightiness and her inability to fend for herself or take anything about life too seriously, had always been able to make me laugh. No matter how hungry I was or now annoyed I'd been at her tendency to act like my sister rather than my mom—and my little sister at that—she'd always been able to make one snide comment and send me into fits of giggles. It was one of the things I loved the most about her. She was constantly getting into trouble but always made me feel lighter when I was with her.

And I hadn't talked to her since I'd arrived in Minneapolis. It was going on two weeks, now, and though I'd been avoiding calling her on purpose, not knowing how it was going to go, I missed her terribly.

I left the library and slid my feet into my flip-flops, my mind distracted from Leo and the dinner we were going to be going to tonight. There was a pay phone right across the street, and I had a call to make.

I just hoped my mom was the one who answered the phone this time. Because I really didn't feel like living through another run-in with Roger.

. . ⚜ . .

I PUT THE RECEIVER to my ear and held my breath, praying like mad that it would be my mother on the other end of the line and not Roger.

Please let it be Mom, please let it be Mom, please let it be Mom, I chanted in my head.

Please don't let it be Roger, with more of his threats and his demands that I return home and face him for whatever it was he thought I'd done.

"Hello?"

The voice took me all the way back to my childhood, when I'd listened to her answering the phone in our tiny apartment and tried to sound as grown-up and cheery as she always did, and my heart froze... and then started hammering away behind my ribs, my eyes suddenly full of tears.

"Mom?" I whispered.

"Oh my goodness, Liv?" she whispered back. "Is that you? Are you okay? What happened to you? Where'd you go? Are you safe, baby girl?"

The feel of being a little girl and looking up to my mom tripled, and I almost had to sit down on the sidewalk with the sudden weakness of my knees. I hadn't realized how much I'd missed her until I heard her voice again.

"I'm fine," I said, trying to get my voice to work the way it was supposed to. "I had to leave town, though. It wasn't..." Shit, how to explain this? How to explain that the guy she'd chosen to stay with had actually threatened my life? "I didn't think I could stay after Roger heard what I said."

She hissed out a breath, and I could just imagine her looking over her shoulder, checking to see whether there was anyone else with her in the kitchen, where they kept the phone.

"It's not just that," she whispered, her voice so quiet I could barely hear her. "Honey, he's positive that you actually took money from him."

Wait, *what*?

"Money?" I asked, too shocked to do anything more than repeat what she'd just said. "What are you talking about? Does that man even have money to take?"

"Now, Olivia, that's not nice," she said, her tone stern. Like I was the one who had been doing wrong here.

And just like that, all the joy I'd felt at hearing her voice again flew right out the window, and my defenses came up. "Neither is knocking you down and standing over you shouting, but I didn't exactly see you telling him to play nice when he did *that*."

"That," she said coldly, "was an accident. And it's also not the point."

I ground my teeth, trying to remember why I'd thought that I needed to call her. "What *is* the point, then?"

"The point is, you can't come back here," she whispered, her voice going intense and frightened again. "He had a stack of cash in his bedside table, and it's gone, and he's positive that you took it. He thinks that's the reason you left town in such a hurry and without saying goodbye."

"I left without saying goodbye because I knew you'd try to stop me," I told her coldly. "And I was going to stay when Roger had called specifically to threaten me over what I'd said to you. Staying wasn't an option. Neither is coming back."

The story didn't make any kind of sense. If Roger had a stack of money, as my mom said, he hadn't come it by any honest means. As far as I could tell, he hadn't worked since he first moved in with my mom. Instead, she'd been working several jobs just to keep a roof over their heads.

And getting beat up for her trouble, though I wasn't sure I wanted to bring that up again. She certainly didn't sound like she was in any mood to be rational about it.

"I don't believe Roger had any money to start with," I told her bluntly. "And if he did and he lost it, that's his problem, not mine. I didn't take anything. I barely took anything from my own house."

"I know, honey. I never thought you did. But he's... he's furious."

And right there, her voice changed again, and I could hear the terror in it. The absolute, bone-shaking fear of the man she was talking about.

Dammit. How many times had he knocked her down and told her she didn't have what it took to get back up again?

"Mom, when are you going to leave that asshole?" I asked quietly. "You don't deserve that. You deserve a man that will take care of you."

A long pause followed, and just when I was starting to think she wasn't going to answer me at all, she said, "Never. I'll never leave him. I love him, Olivia, and that sort of love doesn't just grow on trees. Besides, what would I find if I left? I'm not as young as I used to be, and I can't do half the things I used to do. I'm not exactly a catch these days."

I closed my eyes in a combination of disgust and horror, hearing her repeating things I knew he must have said to her... and hearing the belief in her voice. He'd told her she wasn't worth anything, and she actually *believed* him.

I'd already wanted to kill him, but if I hadn't, that would have driven me over the edge. My mother was a lot of things: flighty, terrible with money, impossible when it came to judging someone's character. She definitely hadn't been cut out to be a mother. But she was also the sweetest, most straightforward person I knew. She wouldn't have hurt a fly if she had a choice.

And she was worth a million Rogers. Only he'd convinced her that she wasn't.

It broke my freaking heart.

And for that reason, I didn't tell her that I'd seen Mark Parker on the street in front of Leo's building. I didn't tell her that I was safe or that I was working or that I had someone taking care of me—at least for the time being. I didn't tell her that I could get to her in hours if she needed me to.

I told her I loved her and hung up very gently, because if my mom was still on Roger's side, it meant I couldn't trust her with anything that he might use to track me down. Particularly if he'd now decided that I had stolen money from him.

CHAPTER 17

LEO

WHEN WE GOT TO MY PARENTS' apartment in the city—a small but extremely classy place in a very good building—Olivia looked up at the art nouveau-style architecture, took a deep breath, and cast a glance at me from the corner of her eye.

"Is it just the four of us tonight?"

I returned the glance, surprised. "I think so. Why, does that matter? Are you secretly harboring a crush on one of my brothers? Because I've got to tell you, it wouldn't be the first time. But neither of them is what I would call relationship material."

She snorted at that and looped her arm through mine, shooting me a look that was half sweetness and half sarcasm.

Sort of like her.

"Why would I want to have a crush on either of your brothers?" she asked, all faux innocence. "I think I probably have the best Folley right here."

She cast me a way-too-sweet smile, and I found myself laughing at her antics—while telling my heart, and my cock, to get a hold of themselves and stop overreacting to a joke.

Which it obviously was.

No matter how much my instincts wanted to say otherwise.

I reached down and took her hand, pretending that was part of the joke and hoping she bought it. "Let me guess. No brothers means they'll have more time to focus on you and ask you all those questions you don't want to have to answer."

She squeezed my hand and made a very wry face. "More or less. It's not that I don't like your parents. But I'm not good at lying to people I like."

I kept my mouth shut on the answer that came immediately to mind. Because it seemed to me that she was *very* good at lying to people. As long as she thought something was important enough to lie about.

I didn't say anything like that, though. Just took a step forward toward the building and then through the doors themselves, telling her what I knew about the building and how long my parents had kept an apartment there.

As we rode up the elevator, though, she was still frowning. "Why do they keep an apartment in the city when they have that gorgeous house in the country?"

I grinned. "Well, my dad had it for when he was working, in case he had to stay overnight or for the weekend or anything like that. They could have sold it when he retired. But I think they keep it so they can come stay in the city and call it a vacation while keeping an eye on me."

We were both laughing at that when the elevator got to their floor, and by the time we got off the elevator and walked to their door, Olivia's hand had relaxed in mine. When my mother answered the door and pulled Olivia in for an immediate hug, one glance at Olivia's face told me that she'd gotten her mask on just in time and was no longer the girl who had stood on the sidewalk outside, questioning herself.

She was now Professional Olivia, the girl who knew exactly who she was and how to play it.

I just wished I knew which of those was the real Olivia.

· · ∼∞∼ · ·

MY MOM LEANED FORWARD, her fork paused over her plate. "Olivia, I've heard that you're not going to work for my son anymore. What gives?"

She actually caught Olivia, who had been in the middle of one of my dad's stories, by surprise, and she turned toward my mother with her mouth open. "What?" she gasped.

My mom smiled a little, pleased at having caught her off guard. "Why did you quit Folley? I've heard nothing but how brilliant you are. Get a better offer? Anything we should be concerned about?"

She twirled a forkful of spaghetti gracefully and popped it into her mouth while I nearly choked on the sip of champagne I'd just taken.

My father was the one who had started the company, and he was the one the world knew as the head of the Folley family. But the world didn't realize that my mother was the one who pulled most of the threads. She just kept her actions behind the scenes, so no one suspected her.

Honestly, she and Olivia probably had that in common. Always underestimated... and always three steps ahead of the opposition.

Olivia, for her part, collected herself quickly and gave my mom a quick grin. "It turns out the board isn't so keen on your son hiring the girl he's currently dating to run his accounting department. And I can't say I blame them. I'm also not going to stand there and act like I don't know what's going on when the board is screaming at Leo about my lack of qualification."

My mom, her mouth still full, just waved this off as completely unimportant, and to my surprise, my dad took up the call.

"But Leo should have told you that the board doesn't get any say in the staffing of the company," he said, his deep voice rumbling with dissatisfaction at this apparent spot on my record. "They don't get to say who comes and goes. And they certainly don't get to fire someone who's doing such a good job."

Olivia turned to him, looking both shocked and betrayed—and more than a little bit comical—as he joined the fray. "Et tu, Brute?" she asked archly.

He shrugged and gave her a quick, unapologetic grin. "Hey, I call them like I see them. I've heard about the work you've been doing in that department, and I've even seen some of it. Leo sent it over to make sure you were right, because you'd blown right past him, and I have to say, I was incredibly impressed."

Now those large, green, and very betrayed eyes were turned to me, and I was shaking my head and defending myself. "Hey, it's still my dad's company at heart. I wanted him to see how good a job you were doing."

The eyes narrowed as Olivia tried to decide whether I was telling the truth or not. "Are you sure? Or do you still turn all the hard questions over to your dad?"

"Well, only the *really* hard ones," I clarified. "But in this case, I was absolutely bragging. Not asking him to solve anything."

Her face cleared as she decided to believe me, and she turned back to my parents. "That doesn't change the fact that he's already lost one investor because of me. I'm not going to keep pushing it."

"If you're good at your job, you keep it," Mom said firmly. "Regardless of what Mr. Burns thinks. I never liked him much, anyhow. Way too stuck up."

Olivia's laughter rang out at that, and she nodded. "He definitely seems to think very highly of himself. But—"

Mom's hand went up, imperious and full of expectations. "Enough. You keep working there. It makes the best sense for the company. Besides, I like seeing you with Leo. I've never seen him as relaxed as he is when you're around. And that's worth the entire board, as far as I'm concerned. Get rid of them all. We'll go private again."

She twirled her fork in her pasta and shoved the bite into her mouth again, one eyebrow rising as she challenged Olivia to find a problem with what she'd just said.

Olivia, however, was blushing so red that I could hardly tell her skin from the bright pink blouse she'd worn today. And when she turned to me, her eyes were full of shock. Shock and... tears.

Was she... crying?

"Mom, stop," I said, half-embarrassed and half-horrified. It had been years since my mom had gone out of her way to embarrass me in front of a girl. And back then, it had been my date to the prom.

Not nearly as important—or as sensitive—as Olivia.

My dad's hand snaked out to catch Olivia's, and I could see him squeezing in encouragement. "Don't take it personally. We've never seen him so happy, and it means the world to us. We just don't want to see him lose that glow."

Her face nearly melted at his words, and I could almost see the thoughts flying through her brain. My parents had never been shy about showing their love for me and my brothers, and it must have been a far cry from what she'd experienced as a kid.

A dad who had left young. A mom who didn't sound like she'd done much to support her daughter. And a flight from her hometown without money because of her mom's new boyfriend. What did she think of my family? A dad who was actually around... and so intent on seeing his sons happy?

• • ⚜ • •

BY THE TIME WE GOT home, we'd both had far too much to drink and had stayed far later than we meant to. We were also talking more freely than we ever had before, and as we stumbled into the apartment, trying to support each other and mostly failing at it, I realized that this might be the ideal time to try to learn more about her. I'd been thinking about her childhood since earlier and had remembered yesterday, when I'd looked down and seen Olivia running into Mark Parker on the street. The way she looked up at him like he was the last person in the world she wanted to see.

The way he'd glowered after her as she walked away.

That had been more than just a stranger on the street, asking for directions. There had been recognition on both sides. And somewhere between her looking at my dad like he was the bees' knees and wishing I knew more about her, I'd remembered that she'd told me that her real name was Olivia Parker.

And she'd then run into Mark Parker and lied to me about who he was.

Yes, it was a very common last name. But she'd come from a small town within driving distance of Minneapolis and had said her dad didn't live in the town where she grew up.

Could it be?

"My dad is in love with you," I told her, depositing her onto a couch in the living room.

"He's in love with *you*," she corrected me. "He'd do just about anything for you, I think."

I shrugged. "Not anything. He refused to buy me a pony when I was a kid, no matter how many times I asked."

She laughed but then grew sober. "At least you know him."

Okay, that was a leading statement if I'd ever heard one. "Do you... Do you know who your dad is?"

Her eyes hardened, the planes on her face suddenly growing sharp. "Nope. He left before I was born."

Well, I'd wanted an opening. Here it was. "Do you... *want* to know who he is? I have a very good PI. I could put him on the case."

"The one you asked to look into my background?" she asked, still sharp. "I'd rather not. Thanks anyhow."

She got up and left before I could respond to that, and I let her go. I was very close to falling asleep anyhow, and it didn't take a genius to figure out that she didn't want company right now. I hoped she'd go to her room and fall asleep quickly.

I hoped she wouldn't remember in the morning that I'd asked her if she wanted me to find her dad for her.

But as I was waiting to go into the hall toward my own bedroom, I pulled out a phone and did a search on Mark Parker. When the results came up, I picked a very young picture of him and enlarged it.

Then I looked at it for at least ten minutes, trying to see Olivia in his face.

I couldn't, but that didn't mean anything. If she was his daughter, I needed to know, because it would change everything.

And with that in mind, I pulled up an email, addressed it to my PI, and started typing.

If she was connected to Mark Parker, and she had any allegiance to him, then I most definitely needed to know about it. Because Burns quitting wouldn't make me want to fire her. But finding out that she was related to my biggest competition—and the guy trying to force me to sell my company—just might.

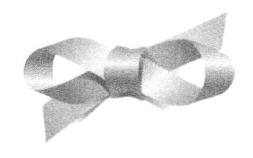

CHAPTER 18

OLIVIA

I WAS IN THE LIBRARY browsing the stacks for what had to be the fiftieth time and marking the books that I wanted to read and didn't think I should actually touch, when I realized something.

I was *bored*.

It had only been two days since I'd walked out of Leo's building, positive that I was doing the right thing, and come home to think about whether or not I should be working there. I'd thought about it a ton but hadn't made my mind up yet, and since then, I'd been stuck in the apartment by myself.

It. Was. Horrible.

And I was bored. There was only so much reading a girl could do, and I didn't want to go shopping again or watch TV or go to a movie or anything else. No, I wanted to use my brain. I wanted to *work*.

This was definitely a problem I hadn't considered when I got on my high horse and walked out of Folley. Don't get me wrong; I still definitely thought I'd done the right thing. If Folley was going to get into trouble for anything, I didn't want it to be for something I'd done—or someone I'd supposedly been seeing. I didn't want other people in the office to think I was a bad influence on Leo himself, and I didn't want any of the other employees thinking they should start dating just because they thought Leo and I were.

But.

I was stuck with Leo for several more days if I wanted to fulfill the contract we had together, and I was starting to realize that it was a whole lot more fun going into the office and using my brain than sitting around here and letting that brain go to waste.

I left the apartment, threw myself onto my bed in my own room, and called Alice. Yes, using the cell phone I'd told Leo I would never use unless I had to. That was how desperate I was for entertainment.

"Let me get this straight," she said, doing her level best to sound serious after I'd explained to her what the problem was. "You have a ridiculously gorgeous guy letting you stay in his ridiculously gorgeous penthouse apartment. He's willing to buy you whatever you want, pretty much whenever you want, and you've got a fully stocked kitchen to boot? And you're complaining because...?"

"I'm booooored," I groaned, drawing the word out and making it in a whine worthy of the whiniest fourteen-year-old girl ever born. "I didn't realize how nice it was to be using my brain until I stopped using it. And I've gone through the entire library and read what I wanted already."

"Guess it's not that impressive, then, is it?" she asked. "And here I was thinking it was big and long and satisfying."

My mouth quirked at the obvious sexual reference, but I wasn't going to let her sidetrack me. "It's not about size, Al. It's about how you use it, and you know it. But that doesn't change the fact that I've already been through the books I want to read."

"So go out and do something. Go to the park. Go to the zoo. Take a class."

Take a class.

Now that was an idea.

I was in a really big city that had at least two community colleges. Why not take a class, improve my education, and give myself something to do?

Then I remembered what classes had been like. Yeah, I'd left NYU because my mom had called me and told me she needed me at home, pronto. But it hadn't been hard when I'd been bored out of my mind sitting in class every day and doing homework all night.

"I'm not going to take a class," I said firmly. "I'll just be even more bored. Worse, they might check into my background and give Roger a way to find me. Besides, it's not like I'm going to be here much longer. Only until the end of the week."

Alice didn't even pause before she bit on that one. "So you're still planning on leaving? Even though you're obviously in love with Leo?"

"What?" I gasped.

"Obviously. In love. With Leo," she said, speaking slowly.

For a moment, I was so shocked that I lost the ability to speak.

Then it came back again.

"Have you been drinking or something?" I snapped. "What the hell makes you think *that*? He's just a guy I'm doing a favor for."

"Oh, I see," she said. "So that must be why you went out of your way to step in and help at his company when the other guy quit. And why you agreed to stay an extra week even though you didn't have to because you'd already satisfied the first promise you made. And why you're so worried about saving his company, even though you won't be there after the end of the week to even know whether it keeps ticking or not. And why you can't stop talking about him every time you call."

I narrowed my eyes at the vision I had of her in my head, all holier than thou and condescending, like she always was when she decided she knew better than me. "First of all, I stepped in to help because that's what any decent person would do. And staying an extra week was the same. He had another engagement, and he really needed someone to help him cover it. The man's been giving me free room and board and paying me to keep him company. He's a good guy. What kind of monster would leave him high and dry when he needs a..."

"Handy-dandy girlfriend?" she supplied.

"No! A friend. That's all. That's all we are. Friends."

"Friends who sleep together. Friends who don't talk about their feelings because they're both more than a little bit in love and neither wants to admit it to the other. That sort of friends?"

Oh, the girl was cheeky. And the bigger problem was that she knew she could get away with it. Of all the people in the entire world, she was the only person who would have dared to talk to me like that.

Because she knew I couldn't stay mad at her for more than five minutes.

"Look, Al," I said, making my voice sound as reasonable as possible. "I know you must have this great romantic idea of what Leo and I are doing, but I promise you're wrong. We're friends. Partners in crime, sort of. Partners who aren't going to see each other again after Sunday. I only have to stay that long, and I'm bored."

"Then go back to work for him again," she replied, and dammit, I was starting to think she'd actually had this entire conversation laid out in her head before we even started talking. How the hell did she have her answers so easily available?

"Did you miss the part where I can't work for him because his board is threatening to quit over our supposed relationship?"

"No, but I also didn't miss the part where you're not planning to be there past Sunday and you're bored. So if you're just friends and you truly don't care about him as anything more than that, screw the board, and screw the risk. Go back to work. Entertain yourself until you have to leave."

Well, shit. When she put it that way, it made it awfully hard to condone staying away. If I was truly leaving at the end of the week, what did it matter? It was only a couple more days.

"I know he already put ads up about the position," I said, pulling on my last excuse. "He's probably already given the position to someone else, and I don't want to pull it away from someone who deserves the job. After all, it's not like I need it."

"But you do deserve it. Hasn't everyone told you already that you're good at it? What are you doing, trying to get more praise from the one person at the office who hasn't praised you enough? Or are you just trying to make Leo realize how much he's going to miss you when you're gone?"

My mouth actually snapped shut at that, because I hadn't even considered it.

But Alice had always been able to see right through me. Was it possible she was seeing something I didn't even realize I was doing?

A quick search of my brain, though, and all of my possible motivations, and I knew she wasn't. I wasn't trying to make Leo jealous by threatening to leave. I *had* left because I didn't like the idea of doing damage to his company by staying.

"You are insane," I said, being just as blunt as she was. "I don't want to make him jealous. I don't want to stay, and I don't want him searching for me after I leave. The more he searches, the more he'll open himself up to Roger, and if Roger does something to Leo because of me, I don't think I could stand it."

"Yep, definitely not in love with him," she said, as if she was answering a question we'd been asking or something. "Definitely no feelings whatsoever."

"Definitely not," I agreed. "The truth is, I'm not even positive that I want to be in accounting. Sure, I'm good at it. But it's not exactly... scratching that itch."

"Does Leo scratch that itch?"

I burst out with laughter. "Alice! Behave yourself!"

"Okay, okay," she said, giggling. "So if you don't want to do accounting, what do you want to do? And are you going to stay in Minneapolis to do it?"

I thought about it for a second. What did I want to do? And was the city the best place for it? Would I stay here—without staying with Leo or having any contact with him—to do my own thing?

"You know, I think I would," I told her slowly. "I like the city. I like the opportunity. I want to... I think I want to start my own thing here."

"I wouldn't put it past you," she said, immediately faithful and on board. "So what do you want to do? Fashion?"

"No way. That's not me."

"Sales?"

It seemed like a good fit, particularly with my knack with numbers, but still...

"No. Something more personal. Something that I can really dig my teeth into."

"Food?"

I tipped my head. I hadn't thought about it, but...

"You know, maybe. Maybe a bakery. And a café. Combined. A place where you could get the most delicious croissants known to man and the best cup of coffee in the city. With a book. I want a bookstore attached to it!"

Another giggle from Alice, but this one was more considering. "I think you maybe start with one and grow," she observed. "The bakery first? Or the café?"

"Yes," I said, my imagination starting to rise up. I could see the place now, all large windows and red striped awnings. Wait, make that green. Script hand-painted across the front to advertise today's specials, which would change halfway through the day.

"And what would you call it?"

"Olivia's," I said simply. "I always think the best restaurants just have one name."

"So do it," she said, her statement just as simple. "Finish this thing with Leo and then get a place of your own and figure out how to make Olivia's a real place."

"As if it's that easy," I said with a laugh.

"I have faith in you," she said. "I also have to run. Are you going to be all right tonight by yourself?"

I told her that I thought I would probably survive and hung up the phone with a promise to call again soon. When I looked to my left, I was surprised to see Leo himself standing in my doorway.

"What are you doing home so early?" I asked, yanking myself up off the bed and turning toward him—while trying to remember whether I'd put any makeup on this morning.

He shrugged. "Came home early. There's a girl staying in my apartment that I wanted to see. Who were you talking to?"

"Alice."

"So, a bakery and a café? And a bookstore? Or did she talk you out of trying all three at once?"

Part of me wanted to be angry that he'd been listening to my conversation. But the other part of me... wanted to hear what he had to say about my idea. He was, after all, the biggest and most successful businessman I'd ever met.

"Maybe," I said with a shy grin. "I'm not sure. But I think maybe."

He nodded like this was the most rational thing in the entire world. "You could do it in a heartbeat. You're so good with numbers, you'd be a natural business owner. And I bet you'd have the best croissants this side of the Mississippi. Whatever that means." He gave me a considering look, his head slightly cocked, and then nodded. "I'd help you, you know. If that's what you want, I'd help you start it. If you wanted help, that is."

I paused, half a smile on my face, and stared at him. Was he being serious right now? Of course I wanted his help.

And of course I knew I couldn't accept it.

That didn't change the fact that I'd never had anyone offer such a thing to me before. I'd never met anyone who cared enough about me to want to help me achieve my dreams.

I'd never met anyone I cared about that much, either.

And I didn't know how to handle it.

CHAPTER 19

OLIVIA

I WATCHED LEO STAND abruptly from the breakfast table, grab his briefcase, and walk out, still on the call he'd taken in the middle of our conversation, and frowned.

I mean, it wasn't like I expected a kiss goodbye or anything, but finishing the conversation would have been… polite. In fact, now that I thought about it, I didn't think he'd ever just stood up and walked away in the middle of a conversation. Yeah, there were times when he got phone calls that he had to take, and he might have to put our talks on hold for a minute while he did business of one sort or another.

But he always at least let me know that that was what was going on. He never just stood up and left. And didn't come back.

I heard the click of the elevator doors sliding shut, though, and then the ding that meant it was descending, and guessed that meant he had, in fact, just stood up and left, without bothering to come back.

"Never should have told him about the bakery," I said, rising from the table and taking my half-eaten bagel with me as I moved into the living room. "That's what I get for sharing my dreams with people I've only known a week and a half."

I dropped onto the couch, grabbed the remote, and started surfing through the new crime channel's offerings, wondering if there were any good serial killer shows I hadn't seen yet.

"Only four more days," I murmured to myself. That final event was this weekend, and I'd promised to stay for that.

And then I'd be gone with the wind and doing something new—which would, I hoped, at least involve getting to use my brain more than I was currently doing.

And yes, in case you're wondering, that meant I had decided not to take Leo up on his offer to help me start the bakery, for all the same reasons I'd already decided on. All the reasons that made it obvious to me—no matter how many times I went through it—that the sooner I was gone from this place, the better.

Because the sooner I was gone, the safer he'd be.

And if he was going to start acting all weird every time we were together, it was just going to make it even easier to leave without giving him a forwarding address.

"ARE YOU CALLING TO finish the conversation we were having this morning when you got up and walked away without saying anything to me?" I asked, answering the phone with that rather than the standard greeting.

I heard an embarrassed groan on the other end of the line.

"I'm so sorry," Leo muttered. "It was a call I hadn't wanted to get—especially before I'd had enough coffee—and the news was just as bad as I'd feared. I guess it took over my body and forced me to walk out without a goodbye."

I whistled. "That must have been some pretty strong news. What happened?"

"That's actually what I'm calling you about. The news was that the person we offered the accounting job to decided to pass, and there's no one else on our list. We got so many of the same applicants as we had before, and the new applicants weren't much better."

"And that was upsetting enough that you left half of your breakfast in the kitchen?" I asked, frowning. That didn't seem like it could have been newsworthy, honestly. Surely Janice, his assistant, had been keeping him constantly updated on the search.

"The upsetting part was that the guy we wanted turned us down," he muttered. "And he was really our only hope."

"So you're calling me because... you're going to send me to his house to talk him into accepting?" I asked, still completely mystified as to why this had anything to do with me.

He laughed. "I'm calling you to beg, on my knees, for you to come back."

Everything inside my body—all those vital organs that kept me ticking—immediately stopped doing what they were supposed to be doing, frozen with...

Frozen with what?

Disappointment, I thought, identifying it quickly. Disappointment and something awfully close to horror at the thought of going back into that building.

"And I already told you that I wasn't going to set foot in that office again, I think," I said quietly. "I gave you my reasons for quitting, Leo. They haven't changed."

He blew out a slow breath, like he was preparing himself for something, and then said quietly, "Olivia, I'm begging you. And I never beg. We haven't been able to find anyone, and we're getting very, very far behind on some really important numbers. The people who were directly underneath you are doing their best, but they're not as qualified as you are, and they're certainly not as creative. Without someone to lead the team, at least for a day, we're going to miss our quarterly numbers. And those numbers are more important than I can tell you. Please."

I bit my lip, taking in the pleading sound of his voice and the situation he'd managed to get himself into—or rather, the situation I'd put him in, since I was the one who'd up and quit without any notice whatsoever. And as I was going through all that, I realized that he'd offered this for a day. Not the rest of the week. Not a month.

A day.

"You only need me for a day?" I asked breathlessly. "A day, and then I'm free again?"

Yes, it sounded stupid. I'd been so excited about working and using my brain, and now I was making it sound like going back would be the equivalent of going to jail. And I did want to go back to work. Work of some type.

But getting out of the numbers game and actually thinking about doing something else—something that required more art and less math—seemed to have turned a switch in my head.

I wasn't entirely sure I wanted to turn it back.

"Just a day," he said, already sounding more relieved. "You're right. I've heard your reasons, and though I don't agree with them, I know you're set on quitting. I know you well enough to know you're not going to change your mind. But we have to get those quarterly numbers organized so they look the way I need them to look, and I'm not sure we can do it without you. I just need a day, Olivia. Please."

Now, I don't know if you've ever experienced it, but having the guy you're sort of completely falling for asking you for a favor and then actually begging you for it...

It's pretty much impossible to say no to.

Besides, there was a pretty big part of me that was shooting off like a firework right now at the thought that he needed me that badly and wasn't afraid to say it. That part was also speaking directly to the space in my lower belly, where I was suddenly feeling all sorts of warmth.

"A day," I said quietly. "But only because I care enough about you to want to save you."

"My hero," he murmured, his voice just as intense as mine and his meaning equally muddy.

I had a split-second thought that we both needed to be more careful because we were taking this contract a whole lot more seriously than we should be, and then Leo had jumped right into the details of the day and what he wanted me to work on, and my brain was rapidly filing it all away and into neat and tidy categories for best possible efficiency.

Half an hour later, after a quick shower and some even quicker makeup application, I was calling a car and hitting the button for the elevator to head back to Folley. I was also promising myself that it was only for that day—and reminding myself once more that at the end of this week, I had to leave Folley, this apartment, and the man behind it all in my past and find a place where I couldn't hurt them.

• • ⚜ • •

I GLANCED THROUGH THE files again, my fingers flying over the keys as I swapped from one view to the next and suppressed a shudder.

When Leo said they were behind, I'd thought he might be exaggerating.

He wasn't.

The quarterly numbers were due on Friday if they were going to make the report Leo needed to make, and from what I was seeing, they weren't even close to ready. Nothing had been filed where it needed to be, making it almost impossible to find what you might be looking for at any given moment. The math was off—I could see that with one quick glance—and it looked to me like there were far more employees entered in the system than actually existed in the company.

It would make it look like the company was only doing half as well as it was, and with the board already getting twitchy, this was going to go down about as well as a lead balloon.

"Shit," I breathed, my eyes flashing back and forth as I took it all in, my brain already working feverishly on a way to fix it as quickly as possible.

They still had plenty of time before Friday, if they were really, really careful.

But I knew the people who were now leading the department. And I didn't think they were good enough to carry it off.

· · ⚜ · ·

THE RESTAURANT WAS one of those places where there was barely any light and way too much ambience, and everyone around us was wearing clothes and shoes that probably cost more than an entire month of rent on my apartment back in Sunnyvale.

In short, it was a place where I definitely didn't belong. Yeah, I'd dressed the part in a tiny black dress and heels that were almost beyond my ability to walk in, but that didn't mean this was the worst of place I wanted to hang out. The truth was, the moment we walked in, I started thinking that everyone around us was probably staring at me and thinking that I was some sort of interloper into the lives of the rich and famous.

Which, I guessed, I sort of was.

After all, I was a girl who'd run to Minneapolis from the smallest of small towns. I wasn't rich, and I didn't speak that elevated version of English that the upper class did. I definitely didn't wear shoes that cost hundreds of dollars or dresses that cost thousands.

And yet here I was, doing just that, after having literally stumbled my way into this world via my car and a pay phone, and then… sort of sticking.

Sticking to the man who was now sitting across this entirely too romantic table from me and raising his wineglass for a toast.

"I still can't believe you got everything fixed by the end of the day. And I can't thank you enough."

I made one of those think-nothing-of-it gestures. "Please. I have to go in and save companies like yours all the time. This was just a midlevel catastrophe."

He laughed, but his face turned serious a moment later, all smoke and smolder and haze and sex.

Wait, sex?

I moved my head and looked at him out of the corner of my eye, trying to change my vantage point, but it was definitely still there. The man was practically oozing sex.

What the hell was he doing?

"Olivia," he said, leaning forward and taking my hand.

Oh crap, I thought, *it's gone even more wrong than I realized. This isn't just about him needing me in the office. He's going to do something insane like propose right now.*

Dammit, how had I missed that?

And why the hell did my stomach feel like it had suddenly turned into a balloon at the thought that Leo liked me enough to think he could propose?

"Yes?" My voice came out in a croak. The opposite of sexy.

"Please. I'm begging. Say you'll come back and work for us again. I don't know how we can do it without you."

"What?"

Another croak, and I was starting to wonder if a bullfrog had found its way into my freaking throat. But I was so simultaneously relieved and disappointed that this was still about the job, and so surprised, that I seemed to have lost control over my voice.

He leaned back and cast me a most charming grin. "Are you sure you can't keep working for me? In one day, you've surpassed what everyone else did since you left."

I laughed nervously, mostly to give myself time to actually think about something other than the stupid disappointment crashing through me, and shook my head. "Leo, we've been through this. You need to get someone else. Someone that people don't think you're dating, preferably. Someone who can take over the department and do the job you need them to do. You... are trying to find a replacement, right? This wasn't just all some trick to get me to come back."

He actually looked offended. "As if I would resort to such cheap tricks!"

I stifled the laugh that wanted to come bubbling up. "I don't know, it seems like you just might, if you think your company's well-being is on the line. But the truth is..." I bit my lip, wondering if I actually wanted to delve into the truth with this man I had every intention of leaving in three days.

Then I decided that as long as I was leaving him, there was really no harm in telling him the truth.

"The truth is, since I left that day and started thinking about it, and about what I really want, I'm realizing that corporate America... Well, I don't think it's for me, Leo. I don't think I want the office job or the numbers or the business suits."

He relaxed so subtly that the moment I saw it, I started questioning whether I actually had.

"Then what do you want?" he asked gently.

I hesitated for a split second, but then the warm fuzziness of him asking—and actually caring—wrapped itself around me, and I started talking. I told him that I wanted something where I could have more creativity and fewer rules. Where I could wear jeans or a skirt or my favorite black boots and no one would say anything to me. Where I could design things and make them without having to worry about whether it was going to upset my boss.

I wanted to run my own business, and I didn't want it to be in an office.

"The bakery," he murmured. "Are you set on it?"

"I think so," I answered, my heart thumping away with excitement. "I'm good with numbers, and I'm good with accounting. But I don't think that's what I want to do with the rest of my life. I don't think it's where I want to spend my energy."

"Right," he said quickly. "Then I want to help you. Where do you think you'll set this bakery up?"

I drew back, reminding myself of my earlier lecture.

This wasn't a man I could stay with. No matter how gorgeous or charming or generous he was. The truth was, those were the exact reasons I couldn't stay with him.

"I want to do it on my own," I told him. "And I don't know where I'll put it. Not yet."

His eyes narrowed just a bit, and a shadow crossed his face, like he'd heard something he didn't trust.

But the moment I saw it, it was gone. And I wasn't exactly going to ask him what that had been. Not when I'd already told him that I was still planning to leave, even after all his generosity.

CHAPTER 20

LEO

"ARE YOU SURE ABOUT that?" I asked, feeling like I'd just swallowed about fifty butterflies.

Yeah, I know. Gross. But it was the best metaphor I could come up with.

You don't hear all the time, after all, that your PI has found things he wasn't expecting to find about the girl you'd asked him to look into—who you'd also told was safe from such snooping.

"That's what he said," Janice said firmly. "He said to call him as soon as you got a second but that you needed to make sure you were alone when you called so you could talk freely. Said not to call when you had the subject around you, whatever that means. Said he'll have questions for you and needs you to be able to answer them without pretending that you're not answering them, because that won't be helpful to him at all."

"Right," I said, ignoring her tone, which was both suspicious and judgmental at the same time. "Anything else?"

"That was it, sir. Though I have to remind you that you have a meeting with what's left of the board on Monday to go over whatever the accounting department turns in for the quarter's numbers. Aside from that, I'm done for the day, and you won't hear anything from me until tomorrow."

I bit my tongue to keep myself from saying that after her last two statements, I definitely needed the break. Janice was, after all, the one I'd tasked with keeping me in line. It was literally her job to give me unpleasant news.

But a break from that news sounded... good.

"You have a good night, Janice," I told her, injecting a whole lot of fake warmth into my voice. "I'll talk to you tomorrow."

She hung up without answering that—another of her more charming personality quirks—and I set the receiver down, trying to think past Janice and her mannerisms.

So Pete had something for me, did he? That... wasn't exactly welcome news. Or rather... Well, it was, I supposed, if you were actually counting on the private investigator you'd hired to find things about the person you'd hired them to investigate.

When that person was Olivia Cadwell/Parker, though, and you weren't really sure if you wanted to know what said PI had found, the news definitely came with some very glaring fine print.

I shouldn't have had him look into her at all. I'd known that much right from the start—particularly when I'd promised her not even a week ago that I wouldn't pry into her past any more than I already had, given her fear that it would be dangerous.

I should never have called Pete. I shouldn't have told him to dig deeper, and I definitely shouldn't have told him the new last name she'd given me.

I closed my eyes and let my head drop into my hands, hating that I'd done it even when I knew I shouldn't.

And then I reminded myself that I'd had good reasons for doing it. She hadn't been honest with me, pretty much from the start, and though I knew she had her reasons for that, there was no denying that she'd been putting a lot of people in danger by keeping secrets. She still wasn't being honest with me, because though I might not know what her secrets were, I'd gotten a whole lot better at being able to tell when she was keeping them.

She knew Mark Parker. I'd seen that much on her face. And I was starting to think there was a very good chance that she was actually related to him, though I couldn't see any resemblance in their faces. The fact that they had the same last name, and had happened to run into each other on the street below my office, and the long, searching look he'd sent after her when she'd walked away from him...

It was all way too convenient to just let slide. And I'd been in business long enough to know that convenient very rarely happened. Coincidences did, but not as often as you might think. If it looked like a duck and walked like a duck...

"Quack, quack," I murmured.

But damn, it was really going to suck if she was related to the guy who was trying to take my company from me. It would suck even more if she was some sort of corporate spy, sent by her own father to get inside information on my company.

Though I still couldn't see how that last guess could possibly be true. I'd already confirmed that coincidences very rarely happened, and her managing to catch my attention and secure an offer to live in my penthouse for the week while she posed as my arm candy—while spying for a man who turned out to be her father—would be an awfully big coincidence. An even bigger one if you counted her doing it at the exact moment when Jonathan had quit and I'd needed an accountant. Besides, she hadn't even wanted to work in the office and had done it only as a favor to me. She'd had very good reasons for leaving, and she'd fought me tooth and nail about coming back.

It just didn't match up. There were too many things that could have gone wrong for it to be some sort of real plan.

But I had to know. And that right there was why I wasn't going to give myself too hard a time for having called Pete in once more and told him to get more on the girl.

I wondered what he could possibly have. I hoped he was going to tell me that I was barking up the wrong tree and driving myself crazy over something that was complete fiction.

Before I could figure out whether I thought that was likely or not, though, the woman in question came strolling into my office, all red pumps and black business suit, topped with an unruly topknot that did very little to contain her hair.

"You look like you've had a very long day," I noted.

She made a face at me. "Considering it's the second day in an office I told you I didn't want to come back to, and further considering that I'm trying to save the day by untangling all the knots your staff made in the two full days that I was gone, I think I'm doing okay," she said. "I mean, I still have lipstick on and everything."

"And some incredible shoes," I noted, letting my eyes run down her body to the footwear in question.

The woman might be the daughter of my biggest rival. But she was also drop-dead gorgeous and the most interesting person I thought I'd ever met in my entire life.

She leaned down to catch my eyes, her lips pressed into a thin line. "Excuse me. My face is up here."

I grinned at her, unabashed and unable to help it. The truth was, I loved having her in the office for a second day in a row. I loved knowing that she was just across the floor from me and that I could walk over to her office to ask a question if I needed to. Yes, it was a whole lot about knowing that the accounting department was in responsible and very capable hands.

It was also knowing, though, that Olivia herself was within reach if I wanted to see her. And I was man enough to admit that—though I wasn't going to use it in the argument I was about to present to her.

"I'm glad you stopped by," I said, pulling a pad of paper toward me. "I wanted to talk to you about something. Have a seat."

She lifted her eyebrows in question but sat without argument, which meant she really didn't know what I was about to say. If she'd known, she would have turned around and left. Which was exactly why I hadn't told her.

It was also why I'd put together a really faultless argument. I was hoping to shock her into agreeing before she could say no.

"I know we've already talked about this," I said, writing the number I'd prepared down. "But I want to make you one last offer. One last plea."

"You already know the answer's no," she said, barely waiting for me to finish.

"But you haven't even seen the number yet," I noted. I finished writing and slid the notebook over her, moving my hand just enough to turn it on the way so that it would be right side up when it got to her.

She glanced down, and her eyes went big—which was exactly the point, really. I'd gone out of my way to come up with something ostentatious. Far more than the amount she was currently making. I knew she was on the run and needed the funds to keep herself safe, and though I was hoping that if she decided to stay, she'd stay with me in my penthouse, I'd also figured that I better offer her enough that she could afford her own place if that was how she wanted to go.

So I'd doubled her current salary and then added another $10,000 on top of that.

She closed her eyes and swallowed heavily, like she was trying to keep from throwing up or something, and took a moment of silence. I could only assume that she was going through the pros and cons in her head, trying to figure out whether this was the right move or not.

I hoped she'd come down on "yes."

Then she turned the notebook back around and shoved it back at me.

"No," she said quietly. "It's not about the money, Leo, and you know it. I don't want to be here anymore, and it's not safe for you if I stay. I can't be bought."

Ouch.

"I'm not trying to buy you," I argued, feeling immediately defensive. Saying it that way just sounded so... cheap.

A single elegant eyebrow lifted in disbelief. "Aren't you? You're offering me a whole lot more than you should be, and I'm sure you know that. What exactly did you think was going to happen here?"

"I thought you were going to at least think about it. I thought you'd realize what a good opportunity it was and maybe even think about how much I want you to stay."

She leaned forward and dropped her chin and her voice. "And yet you know I can't. I can't stay here, because working in a corporate setting is eating my soul. And I can't stay with you, because doing so would expose you to dangerous people. I'm not willing to do it. That's my final answer, Leo. I'm sorry you don't like it, but it's not going to change. I just came in to let you know that I'm finished for the day. I've left plenty of notes for whoever comes in to handle things tomorrow. I won't be coming back to the office. Don't ask me again."

And she got up and walked out, her hips swaying in the pencil skirt of her suit and her heels clicking against the linoleum as she left my office for what I thought was probably the last time.

"Dammit," I hissed.

I'd thought she would at least consider it. But I'd also thought that the money would sway her.

Turned out I was wrong on both accounts. And my company—which did desperately need her brain—was probably going to pay the price for my gamble.

CHAPTER 21

OLIVIA

I LEANED BACK AGAINST the door of the bathroom, my eyes on the tub and shower spread out before me and my thoughts on the meeting I'd just walked out of with Leo.

Well, not just walked out of. I'd had to get out of the building and into a car and all the way to the penthouse before I arrived in my bathroom desperate for a bath. But still. The point is pretty much the same.

I couldn't believe he'd offered me more money. I mean, I could. Live your entire life with that sort of money and see what sort of doors it opens and you, too, I suspected, would think it was the answer to any and all problems life might throw your way.

Those of us in the real world, though, on the ground with all the commoners, knew differently. We knew that money wasn't the answer to all problems… and certainly wasn't the way to try to talk someone into staying with you just a little bit longer.

I groaned and slid down the door, coming to rest on my butt. And then I let my face drop down to my knees. And I started crying.

Because I'd known that I was going to have to leave that company. I'd known that I was going to have to leave Leo. It was for the best, all the way around. But there had been a really big part of me that was hoping he'd find a way to keep me there. An argument that I hadn't thought of or some really good reasoning that discounted everything I'd come up with so far. Something that convinced me that I'd be safe in his life—and that he'd be safe with me, regardless of the existence of the Notorious Roger.

I'd been really, really hoping that he'd take me in his arms, hold me close, and tell me that it was all going to be okay and that we'd find a way through it that allowed us to stay in the same place.

No, I hadn't wanted to keep working at his company, but I'd thought there might be an opportunity for me to do my own thing. With his support. I'd hoped that he'd seen how much I wanted to do something else and was already thinking of a way to make that happen.

Okay, sure, it wasn't exactly strong. I'd been quite literally hoping that this man would play knight in shining armor and show me the way out of a mess. I'd even been hoping that he would play a big part in that way out.

Instead, he'd thought he could quite simply buy me off. Offer me more money, and that would make everything go away. Shit, he'd probably thought I'd be so dazzled by the amount that I wouldn't even think twice about agreeing to it.

He'd never considered that I might want more than just money. He'd never even thought that I might have said yes, if he'd offered his partnership and his umbrella of protection. If he'd actually talked to me about the things that I was running from.

Instead, he'd just thought he could buy me off.

I didn't know about the thought process behind it, and I certainly wasn't privy to what he'd expected.

But I knew that the tearing feeling in my gut, the feeling that the balloon of emotions that had been building there had just been cruelly popped... That wasn't a good sign for my heart.

And really, it just confirmed what I'd already suspected. I had to go. I'd already known it, and Leo himself had just confirmed it.

Because it was now looking a whole lot like I had feelings for a man who didn't care one fig about me, except as someone who could help his company pad its numbers for that quarterly report.

I LIFTED MY HEAD UP about fifteen minutes later, telling myself firmly that sitting here on the floor crying wasn't going to solve one damn thing except to make my mascara run and make my eyes puffy, and neither of those was a good look.

I did still want that bath.

But when I looked at the tub in my bathroom, I remembered that although this bath was nice and roomy, there was another bath in this penthouse, and it was nicer and roomier. Plus, it had jets and one of those cool trays where you could set a book and a glass of wine.

Or a bottle.

I got up off the floor, kicked off my shoes, and made for the kitchen.

Five minutes later, I was heading for Leo's bathroom and its enormous tub, a bottle of wine and a glass in one hand and a book—new and totally not collectable—in the other. I'd gone to the elevator and pushed a combination of buttons I'd found yesterday that would mean Leo would have trouble getting up to this floor without a security override, because I wanted some time to myself.

And now I was going to have the bath of the century.

I slid into the bathroom, my eyes on the tub and a grin on my face, and shut the door quietly behind me. Seconds later, I was setting the bottle and glass and book down on the ground to wait for me and going through the endless array of options I'd brought in when it came to bath salts, bubble bath, oil, and the like.

My grin widened as I remembered that this was stuff I'd bought on my first day here, when I didn't know exactly how long I'd been staying and had been intent only on getting clean. I'd bought everything I could think of, courtesy of Leo's account, and I hadn't even considered expense.

Today, I was glad I'd chosen such a wide array of goods.

I picked out peach-scented everything, including bath salts, bubble bath, and oil, and dumped it literally into the water—already running—so that the bubbles would start building. Then I turned the jets on, just for good measure. I had no idea if any of that stuff would hurt the function of the jets, but I figured it would be pretty stupid to make a bathtub into a spa with jets if you couldn't use both functions at the same time.

Then I turned to get undressed and let the bathwater and soap do its job.

By the time I was comfortably situated in the tub, the bottle of wine already uncorked and the book sitting right next to it, the bubbles were nearly at the top of the tub, and the bathroom itself was filled with a hazy, peach-scented mist from the heat of the water.

In short, it was heaven.

I picked up the bottle and awarded myself with a very generous pour, congratulating myself on having picked one of the cheapest books in the library, and then I took a sip of wine and started reading.

Hey, I was in here to get my mind off of Leo and the offer he'd made. I didn't want to have to think about what it meant or what I'd be doing this weekend, when it came time to pack up and go.

I just wanted to enjoy what would probably be my last soak in this particular tub, with hot water that I hadn't paid for and wine that I'd never be able to afford. I wanted to read a book and let it take me far, far away. And when I came back, I'd think about what I wanted to do next with my life and how I was going to get it done.

And this weekend, I'd do that last appearance with Leo, then take the money he owed me and go back to being a lone wolf. I'd always done better on my own.

It was time I remembered that and got back to my roots.

• • ⁂ • •

I HAD FORGOTTEN THAT Leo didn't believe in knocking when he came to a closed door. Especially when that closed door belonged to his bathroom, where he didn't expect anyone to be lounging in the tub, reading a book and halfway through one of his best bottles of wine.

The door opened relatively slowly, at least, but it still scared the living daylights out of me. I jumped and screeched at the sudden movement, which came when I was in a really intense part of the book, and the sudden action sent the wineglass I'd been holding flying. It also sent the bottle of wine and the book right into the tub.

I screeched louder at this, my brain immediately thinking that something bad would happen to me, and jumped up, lifting one foot up to my knee like I could protect it from what I'd just spilled into the water, and looked down, horrified at what I'd done.

The wineglass that I'd practically thrown came to a shattering halt at that moment, ending its life against the tile of the floor and spattering more wine everywhere, and I yanked my eyes from the now-burgundy-tinted bubbles around me to the floor and what had been the wine glass.

"Oh shit," I gasped, looking from the remains of the glass to the rapidly sinking book and now purple bathwater. "Leo's going to kill me."

I ducked down and grabbed at the book, pulling the sopping thing out of the water and setting it quickly on the lip of the tub, then grabbing for the wine bottle.

By the time I got it out of the water, of course, all the wine inside was either gone or heavily mixed with bathwater, and I set it aside with a grimace, very, very sorry to have lost the end of that bottle.

"And that was good wine, too."

At that moment, I remembered what had caused me to waste the wine, and my gaze shot from the ruined bottle up to the door. The door that had opened when it didn't have any business doing so.

Leo was standing there, his arms crossed and his shoulder resting against the doorjamb like he was posing for a calendar or something.

Even worse, he was looking all hot and smoldery again, his eyes on fire and his lips slightly open in a breath.

His fucking chest was even heaving.

And heaven help me, did my body respond to the entire picture, heating right up to boiling point and almost melting with desire at the sight of him.

Then I realized that he was standing there staring at me hopping around in the bathtub naked, while he was fully clothed. I also remembered that I'd already decided that I couldn't get any more involved with him than I already was, as it would just lead to both of us hurting worse when I left.

And I sat quickly back down in the winey tub, telling my libido to get a hold of itself because nothing was happening between Leo and me. Not ever again. He'd already shown me who he thought I was, and I wasn't having it.

"Ever think about knocking?" I asked, cranky at his catching me unawares again.

"I'm pretty sure we've gone over the fact that I don't generally knock when I'm walking into my own bathroom," he said, his eyes dragging up from my now bubble-covered breasts to my eyes. "Are you enjoying yourself?"

"I was," I pouted. "Until you came through the door and made me spill the wine and lose my place in the book."

His eyes went to the book, amused, and then back to mine. "I'm pretty sure you did worse than lost your place. I hope that's not one of my first editions."

I glared at him. "Don't worry. I made sure I picked out something that was published in the last five years. What are you doing home so early?"

He shrugged and wandered in casually like he had every right to be there.

I mean sure, he did. It was his bathroom, after all. But I'd thought that the fact that I was laying naked in his tub might at least mean he had the decency to turn around while I got out.

Instead, he sat down on the edge of the tub, probably ruining his expensive trousers with the water and wine that got all over him. And he didn't even look like he cared about that.

My heart did a little happy dance at the implication that talking to me was more important than his pants, but I pushed it ruthlessly back into place. This was not the time to get all romantic.

This wasn't a romantic situation. Because Leo just thought of me as a sort of employee. Nothing more. Nothing less.

"What's up?" I asked, my voice coming out breathless despite my best attempts to sound just as casual as he looked.

To my complete shock, he bent at the hip and pressed a gentle and very delicious kiss to my lips, pausing to taste me with a flick of his tongue before pulling away.

"I missed you," he murmured. "And I thought I'd come home and treat you to dinner. Then I thought we might be able to talk about that bakery of yours. Though that can wait until you're done with your bath." He frowned slightly at the tub, which now smelled of peach wine, and then offered me a questioning look. "Are you going to... stay in it?"

I made a face. "Not anymore. But I'm not really that hungry. I was actually thinking of just reading in my room and going to bed early tonight. Give me a second, and I'll turn your bathroom back over to you."

I saw the shadow cross his face and the confusion color his eyes, and I knew I sounded abrupt and dismissive. I knew he was probably asking why I suddenly didn't want to hang out with him.

But I also knew that I was going to be gone in a couple of days. And hanging out with him now—or paying too much attention to that kiss he just gave me—would only make the leaving harder. For both of us.

CHAPTER 22

LEO

I DIDN'T SEE HER AGAIN that night. Or the next morning for breakfast.

Yes, I checked to make sure she was still in the house—and in her room. And by "checked," I mean I literally put my ear to her door as I walked by to listen for sounds of movement in there.

Not sexy. Not subtle. More like the actions of a stalker, to be honest. But also completely necessary. After she blew me off in the bathroom and completely refused to have dinner with me—and then didn't show up for breakfast—I was starting to wonder whether she'd decided to leave in the middle of the night, just to avoid the drama of having to say goodbye.

It made sense if she did. I mean, not in a grown-up, *I live an adult life* sort of way, but in the way that it might if she was truly some sort of corporate spy who was secretly working for Mark Parker and had been very nearly found out.

Or, I thought, trying to be fair, if she'd decided that she'd stayed in one place long enough and now needed to keep running but didn't want to tell me that she was doing it, and didn't want to stick around long enough to say goodbye.

Neither of those options was good. Both were trying really, really hard to break my heart.

So I'm sure you can imagine the flood of relief that made my knees weak when I heard her still banging around in her bedroom. And I mean banging like she was building some new furniture in there or something.

I leaned back from the door and stared at it, confused.

I didn't remember buying new furniture that required building, and I didn't remember her asking if she could install new bookcases in a room that didn't actually belong to her.

A room that, as far as I knew, she wasn't planning to stay in for much longer.

The banging stopped abruptly like she'd heard me thinking about it, and I quickly backed further away from the door, turned, and started walking down the hall toward my room again, like it was what I'd been doing right from the start.

If my guess was right, she was already having second thoughts about being here. The last thing I was going to do was let her catch me hanging around outside her door spying on her. Because I was thinking that would just make her leave even faster.

And that didn't fall in line with my plans at all. I wanted the girl to agree to stay. Forever, if possible.

I just had to figure out whether I would still want that after I found out what her relationship was with Mark Parker. And if I *did*...

Well, I had to figure out how to convince her to stay. But that particular problem could wait until after I'd talked to Pete about what he'd found out.

· · ⚜ · ·

I LEANED DOWN AND WROTE a quick note to myself in the file of the girl I'd just interviewed, noting that she was the best of the bunch and was the one I wanted for the job, and then leaned back, feeling very satisfied. That one, I thought. No, she wasn't as sharp as Olivia, but I didn't think anyone would be. No one would be quite as good as the girl who refused to work here any longer.

But this one that just left, Samantha Rivers, was the best I'd interviewed so far, and I thought she'd do just fine, if we could get her. I made another note about the salary I thought we should shoot for—roughly half of what I'd offered Olivia, but that was because Olivia was a special case—and then underlined it three times.

Picking up my phone, I hit the series of buttons that would connect me to Janice's desk.

"Janice," I said when she picked up. "I want that one. Samantha Rivers. Call her and offer her the package I'm emailing you right now. Increase that number in $10,000 increments until she says yes. Let me know how it goes."

I hung up before she could answer, knowing from experience that she'd take care of it and let me know whether it worked or not. Janice was always hanging over my shoulder, pushing me around more than I liked, but she also didn't require much in the way of supervision. She was the epitome of self-sufficient.

Which meant she was the best person to make sure we got Samantha for the position.

"Thank goodness," I breathed.

Finally, someone to fill that position so I could stop wondering how much I could lean on Olivia. And someone to depend on if—and when—Olivia left and I could no longer depend on her.

I looked up just in time to see Jack walking through the door, all smooth grin and swagger, and smiled.

"Found one," I told him immediately. "She's not as good as Olivia, but she's pretty damn good."

"Thank goodness," he said, echoing my statement and dropping into one of the chairs across the desk from me. "I was starting to think you weren't going to be able to find anyone at all."

I leaned back and stared at the ceiling. "You and me both. I've been losing sleep about this every night."

"And yet this was under your control the entire time," he noted. "You don't usually lose sleep over something you know you're handling yourself, Leo. What's going on?"

I didn't answer right away, wondering instead exactly how much I could tell him. Jack was my best friend and my second-in-command at the company, and I trusted him with just about everything.

But a lot of the stuff I'd been thinking about wasn't public information. It wasn't even stuff I'd let out of my head yet. And I wasn't sure I wanted to say any of it out loud, because it would make it a whole lot more real.

I couldn't exactly tell him that I was increasingly attracted to the girl—more so with every time I walked in on her in my bathtub. I couldn't tell him that I was having more and more trouble thinking about her without feeling every sense come suddenly to life, ready and waiting for the feeling of her against my skin.

I definitely couldn't tell him that I wanted her to stay and was feeling more than a little bit lost at the knowledge that she was probably going to go.

And I didn't want to tell him that I suspected her of being related to Mark Parker—and lying about it. Jack was a conspiracy theorist on the best of days. I wasn't going to give him more to guess at, especially when it pertained to the girl I was getting... way too attached to.

"It just feels weird to be replacing Olivia," I finally said, thinking it was not only the truth but also general enough that he wouldn't be able to find anything too suspicious about it. "She's just so good at the job."

"And yet she's right to tell you she can't work here anymore," Jack said immediately. "She's doing you a favor, man. Looking out for you when you're too stubborn to look out for yourself."

Okay, I hadn't thought about it that way. But now that he said it...

Yeah, I could see how she was doing just that. I'd been known to make decisions based on my stubborn idea of how things should be. I'd also been known to sort of collect people who could make up for that particular shortcoming.

I just hadn't expected Olivia to be one of them. And I certainly hadn't been aware that she'd become that sort of ally while I was looking the other way.

"I don't like that it feels like we're giving in to the board," I said. Stubbornly.

"You're not giving in to the board. You're being responsible when it comes to playing with other people's money. And if she doesn't want to work here, you can't exactly make her."

"I'm just afraid that she doesn't want to work here because she thinks she's causing problems, when she's actually not," I added.

"Leo, I don't know the girl well, but I think I can say that if she doesn't want to work here, she's probably got a good reason for it. She's probably thought about it and approached it from all angles and has even run some numbers that you and I have never even considered. She doesn't strike me as the sort of girl who makes decisions without putting any thought into it."

I didn't answer. Everything he was saying was right, and true. Olivia was more capable than anyone I'd ever met, and she definitely wouldn't have pulled the cord on a decision if she wasn't positive about her reasons.

But that didn't mean I had to like it.

• • ⚜ • •

WHEN MY PHONE RANG and I glanced at the screen, I saw the picture I'd saved of Mark Parker.

I cringed but hit the button to accept the call and put the phone to my ear.

"Mark. Pretty sure I told you not to call for another six months. I already gave you my answer."

"Is Olivia Parker working for you?"

I was so surprised I actually jerked back and looked at the phone like it wasn't working right.

"What?" I asked, forgetting everything I'd ever learned about making a business adversary think you already knew exactly what he was going to say.

"Olivia Parker. Is she still working for you?"

I bit my lip and let my brain work for two seconds. This confirmed that they knew each other, which I'd been wondering about. But why the hell was Mark calling and asking something like that?

What was it to him whether Olivia was still working here or not?

"Do you *know* Olivia?" I asked, thinking that I'd use the conversation to do a little research before I gave him any hard answers.

"I may. Ran into her outside of your office. Wondered if she's working for you or if it was just a coincidence."

"She's been working here a little bit," I said vaguely. "But I'm in the process of replacing her."

Mark didn't answer me, and he didn't ask about Olivia again, so that must have somehow answered his question—or giving him more to think about it. Honestly, I wasn't sure which it was.

I also wasn't sure I wanted to know. I'd had enough dealings with Mark to know that he very rarely moved along a straight path and was very, very hard to predict. I'd never made the mistake of thinking that he was aboveboard. Honestly, I thought there was a really good chance that he was involved with the mob.

Of course, that made me even more worried about any possible connection he had with Olivia. She didn't seem like she was involved with that sort of stuff, but she wouldn't have been a very good corporate spy if she made things like that obvious, would she?

"You thought any more about the offer?" he asked abruptly.

"I told you to call me in six months," I responded smoothly. At least this I had an answer for.

An answer I'd already given him in this conversation, though he evidently hadn't been listening to me at that time. Too concerned with asking about Olivia.

"I'd recommend you think about it a little bit more," Mark continued.

Then he hung up without saying anything else.

I stared at the phone again, frowning at the sudden cutting off of the conversation. What the hell had that been? He'd called me just to ask about Olivia and then made an excuse by asking about the offer he'd made on my company, which I'd already told him I wasn't going to accept?

Why?

What was it to him if she was working here? And why had telling him that I might be getting rid of her caused such a strange reaction?

I'd thought there was a chance that they were related. Maybe she was his daughter and was here doing research for him—or worse. But the way he'd acted, the way he'd sounded so possessive, and the way he'd taken it personally that I was replacing her...

It made me think this was a whole lot more than just a father/daughter relationship.

What if it was way more? What if Parker wasn't her maiden name at all, but the name she took after she married Mark Parker himself?

I needed to ask her. I needed to get right to the bottom of this and ask *her* rather than making all these insane assumptions. It was probably the only way I'd find out what was actually going on.

But I didn't know how I'd ever bring that up. How, exactly, do you say that you suspect the girl who's been living with you of being a corporate spy, related to the man who's trying to pressure you into selling your company?

You don't. Not unless you're ready for any relationship you had with her to be over.

And I wasn't. Not even close. Which was why I decided to wait to hear what the PI had to say, rather than taking it to Olivia.

Besides, I wasn't sure whether she was even talking to me at this point, anyhow.

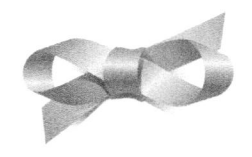

CHAPTER 23

OLIVIA

I WAS IN THE MIDST of doing my last load of laundry in a whole morning of doing laundry, because when you have access to a free and available washing machine and you're not having to worry about someone leaning over your shoulder, breathing down your back and taking sneak peeks at your undergarments as you wash them, you take advantage of it.

Especially when you don't know where you'll be at this time next week or whether you'll still have access to a washing machine. Or even a room of your own.

The problem was, of course, that I had zero idea what I was going to do after I was finished with the laundry. It had kept me pretty busy all morning, but now I was on the last load—and that was including all the towels I'd used this week, both in my bathroom and in Leo's. I'd even washed his towels, much as I hated the way it looked.

Just to have something to do.

Of course, in between, I was daydreaming about what I could be doing at this time next week, or this time next month. The idea of the bakery had taken root in my head and stuck, and I'd now not only named it but also started coming up with a menu—which might change weekly, I thought. Not with big changes, but with little additions and specials that you could only get for the week. Things that made it new and different. Special.

Things that would make for repeat customers. After all, if you ordered the special one week and liked it, chances were pretty freaking good that you'd come back the next week to see what the new special was. I thought that people probably returned for their favorites, but that they'd also return for variety. Fresh new things that they'd never had anywhere else—and that they didn't know if they'd be able to get in two weeks.

It would be like a choose-your-own-adventure eating experience.

I marked that down in my mental database to explore later for possible names and then dove into another idea. If people liked a specific special enough, they'd want to get it again, and it might not be good to just tell them that they wouldn't be able to.

I needed to find a way to make it less black and white. Less stark.

A secret menu, I realized immediately. If I kept the specials around but kept them off the menu, so that people who'd ordered them before could ask for them again, but only because they knew they'd once existed...

"Brilliant," I breathed, placing my elbows down on the washing machine and resting my chin in my hands. "Completely brilliant. Make people feel included by giving them a secret menu that only they know about. Keep the specials around for people who like them enough and make them part of an exclusive club."

It was so smart I could hardly believe it. And the best part was that I'd never heard of anyone else doing anything like it. Sure, there were restaurants that had secret menus and other restaurants that had endless options for personalizing whatever it was you were getting, but a secret menu that got new items every week, and was available only to people who came back to the bakery again and again?

"It'll have to be more than a bakery, though," I said, continuing my conversation with myself. "A bakery won't be able to give me enough options. A café instead. More food options."

And coffee and drink options, too, I added.

This was brilliant. And I already knew what I was going to do after I was finished with laundry. I needed to get these ideas down on paper and start developing them. Finding the weak places and correcting them and figuring out how I was going to get it all done.

And suddenly, I couldn't wait for the laundry to be finished so I could get started with that brainstorming session.

Of course, life had other plans.

My phone rang from the other room, my favorite punk band blasting out as a ring tone. Dammit. And right when my brain was involved in coming up with something so smart that it might make me millions.

Or thousands.

I dropped the laundry I'd been folding and sprinted for my bedroom, intent on getting to the phone before it stopped ringing. There were only two people with that phone number: Alice and Leo.

I didn't want to miss a call from either of them.

I went skidding into the bedroom, already reaching for the phone, and brought it quickly up to my ear.

"Hello?" I gasped.

"Shit, are you okay? What's going on?"

Leo, then, and he sounded well and truly freaked-out. Possibly because I sounded like I'd just run a marathon.

"Oh, you know. Just doing sprints up and down your hall to keep myself sharp," I huffed. "Don't worry. I'm not actually running from a mass murderer or anything."

"Well, that's good news," he replied, a grin coming through in his voice. "I'd hate to come home and find your blood all over my floor. Messy."

"And inconvenient. I mean, what would you do with the body? And if there was no body, would you report it to the cops so they could search for one? That could lead to difficult questions."

"Things I've never taken the time to think about before," he confirmed. "Which leads me back to being glad that you're just running sprints on your own. Are you... finished with the sprints? Or am I catching you in the middle of them?"

I laughed. "I happen to be at a good stopping point. What's up?"

Yes, I was in the midst of getting ready to leave his house and hadn't yet decided whether I was going to say goodbye to him first. That didn't mean I couldn't enjoy a conversation with him, did it?

No, I wasn't flirting. How dare you?

"I actually need you to come into the office," he said. "I know, and I'm sorry."

This second part came just as I was opening my mouth to remind him that I wasn't working for him anymore, and I rapidly altered my statement. "Miss me bad enough that you're asking me to come visit you at work, now? Desperation isn't a good look on you, Leo."

I said it as a joke, but I heard how it sounded as it came out of my mouth.

It didn't sound like I was joking.

"You have no idea how much I miss you," he replied, and he wasn't joking, either. "But we already know that I'm not going to ask you to stay again. I already hired someone else. I have a meeting with the board this afternoon to let them know, and they'd like to have you there to sign off on her coming on board. Are you game?"

Oh. Right. He'd already replaced me, and they just needed me to sign off on the new employee. Give her my blessing, or whatever. I could do that.

I could also pretend that my heart wasn't breaking right down the middle at the thought of him getting cozy with some other girl. Taking late-night meetings to go over numbers. Congratulating her on saving the company. Taking her to dinner to thank her for a job well done.

Finding out what sort of restaurants she liked best and aiming for those.

I jerked my thoughts out of that particular rabbit hole, gave myself a mental shaking, and forced a grin onto my face. "So suddenly they're interested in my opinion?"

"I am," he said seriously. "And they're smart enough to believe me when I say that you know what you're talking about."

Damn, the man was just full of guilt trips today.

"In that case, I'll be glad to help," I told him. "What time?"

The meeting, it turned out, was at 3:00, and Leo recommended that I dress in a business suit to look impressive. I groaned mentally about that, hating the thought of pouring myself back into one of those skirts, but agreed that I'd be there with bells on, ready to approve the new girl.

Ready to hand the keys to Leo's castle over to a girl who was more willing to stay with him than I was.

I already knew that I was going to hate every minute of it. And that I owed him and would do it no matter how much I hated it.

. . ~ . .

SONYA GREGORY, THE one and only woman on the board and someone who looked like she could take on any of the men and eat them for breakfast with no problem, took my hand and shook it.

"I know this isn't what we wanted, but I think it's the right call," she said.

I squeezed her hand, thankful for the moral support. "Honestly, it's fine," I told her. "I know it hasn't looked great, and it definitely hasn't gone the way I wanted it to. But the truth is, I'm not sorry to be leaving accounting."

We'd just finished the meeting, where I'd told the board that I thought the new girl—Samantha Rivers—would do a great job. She had a solid background and a degree from a very good university, and the references I'd called for her had all given me glowing reviews.

I mean, I hated the girl. I figured her friends probably called her Sam for short, and she probably had the exact right amount of curl in her hair and eyelashes that didn't even need makeup. She probably lived in one of those beautiful apartments that look like they've been done up by a professional interior designer and had exactly the right amount of light. And I was betting she had a cat: long-haired and calico, with a collar that had a tag with her name on it.

But all of that aside, I was betting she'd do a great job. Leo wouldn't have hired her otherwise. And the board had agreed, most of them listening to my recommendation and then filing out before they had to talk to me. Sonya was the one and only holdout, and I still wasn't sure why she'd stuck around. It wasn't like we'd built a close relationship in the time I'd been here or something.

This was actually the first time I'd ever even talked to her.

The woman in question lifted one perfect auburn brow—which matched her straight, perfect auburn french twist so perfectly that I thought she was either a natural redhead or had the best hairdresser/eyebrow artist ever—and cocked her head at me. "You don't like accounting? But I've heard you're the best at it."

I tipped my own head back and forth, indicating that she might be right about that. "I'm pretty good at numbers, yeah. But it's not what I want to do. Not anymore. So I'm not sorry to be leaving the position, especially if it helps Leo."

She skipped right over that last part. "If you don't want to do this, what do you want to do?"

I pondered that for a moment, wondering if it was a real question or just something she was asking to be polite. The woman was about ten years older than me, so not outside of the realm of believability when it came to a friend, but she had to be rich beyond my wildest dreams to be sitting on the board of a company like Folley.

Why did she care what I wanted to do with my life?

Still, I didn't have a lot of friends, and the thought of talking about it with someone who wasn't Leo was...

Too tempting to pass up.

Before I knew it, Sonya and I were sitting at the table again, our heads leaning close to each other as I rapidly went through what I'd already decided and what I was thinking. I told her about the bakery and how it had already developed into a café, and what I wanted to do with the menu and how I thought it would affect the clientele and how they felt about the place. I was talking about the name I'd decided on and how I thought I'd want to decorate it and how it wanted it to eventually also have books so that people could come and eat and read and maybe even have meetings or book clubs or author appearances or anything else of the sort.

And to my extreme surprise, Sonya, the woman who had to have millions in the bank and a ton of business experience, lit up with excitement at the idea, jerked a notepad toward her, and started jotting more notes, asking me what I thought about this and that and how this might help the whole idea.

And I was having so much fun that when her phone rang and we realized that two hours had passed, I was actually sorry to cut the conversation short... and was quick to agree when she suggested that we meet for a late coffee tomorrow to continue with the brainstorming.

CHAPTER 24

LEO

I STUCK OUT MY HAND, waiting for Samantha to accept it.

"We're so happy to have you on board, Samantha," I told her, meaning every word of it. "I think you have exactly the sort of experience we've been lacking, and though you've never managed a department as large as this one before, I have zero doubts about you being able to do it."

She smiled and did a sort of sparkle thing, her teeth very bright white and her eyelashes so long that I wondered if they were actually real. The girl was beautiful, that much was certain. And very talented, and, I was hoping, equally motivated.

She was nothing compared to Olivia. But that particular ship had sailed, and I was working very hard to be satisfied with what I had instead of pining after the girl who didn't want to work for me.

"Please call me Sam," Samantha said, taking my hand and shaking it firmly. "And I'm excited to be here. You've already been more than generous with the contract, and I think we're going to make a great pair."

A great pair. The way Olivia and I had been?

Obviously not. Because I wasn't dating Samantha. Of course, I also wasn't dating Olivia. Not really. We were just pretending.

Mostly.

At least that was where it had started. And then we'd started falling prey to late-night talks that included too much wine. Whispered jokes in the middle of charity parties. Video game battles that lasted all night and left us both feeling very hungover the next morning.

And in between, stolen kisses and nights spent in bed, wrapped up with one another like we never wanted to separate.

"Mr. Folley?" a voice said, breaking into my daydream.

I jerked back into reality, finding myself not tangled in the sheets with Olivia but actually in my office, finishing an introductory interview where a new employee and I had just signed a contract for her employment. Said employee was sitting on the other side of my desk right now, staring at me like she thought I might have lost my mind, and honestly, I didn't think she was that far off.

My mind had been far, far away from this office, and precisely none of it had been focused on Samantha Rivers or her employment with my company.

It had been remembering the scent of Olivia's skin when I leaned down to press a kiss to the hollow of her belly, my eyes closed with the bliss that came after a night of taking her again and again.

I really had to get my mind in the game. Olivia wasn't mine to think about like that, and even if she was, this wasn't the time or place for it.

"I'm sorry, Samantha," I told her quickly. "I've had a really long week. My brain isn't reacting the way I'd like it to." I gave her a quick, mostly genuine grin, and stood up. "I'd hoped to have the woman who was handling the department in to train you, but that doesn't look like it's going to work out, so I'm afraid we're going to throw you in the deep end to fend for yourself."

She returned the smile. "That doesn't scare me, sir. I'm sure I can handle it."

"Terrific. And don't call me sir. It makes me feel like you should be talking to my father rather than me."

She giggled at that and nodded, then turned and walked out of my office and toward the office that had once housed Olivia, to take over the things that Olivia had handled for too short a time.

Which gave me plenty of time to turn around and stare out the window, giving my brain free rein to think about Olivia.

Not that thinking was giving me any great ideas about what to do with her.

She was still living in my house and would be until we finished our contract, which would be up with the last event this weekend. She'd done what I'd asked her to, improving my own reputation by leaps and bounds just with her presence, and had actually gone beyond that with her efforts in the accounting department. She'd driven her old car right into my life, nearly run me over, and had then changed everything so dramatically that I didn't know if I'd ever be able to put it back the way it was.

I scooted my chair forward and looked straight down at the alley where I'd first met her, remembering those first conversations. That lunch in the diner where I tried to figure out whether she was what she seemed to be or if she was something more. The moment before that, when she almost hit me with her car, and I used it to con her into going to lunch with me. I thought about the moment when I realized that she might be the answer to the problem I had—and that I might be the answer to the problem she had.

Not that she wanted to tell me anything about those problems. No, she'd been a closed book on that particular topic right from the start. Hadn't wanted to give me any information whatsoever, and had actually gotten more and more defensive the more I asked.

All of which led me back to where we were now.

The girl had lied to me about her last name and hadn't told me why. She hadn't told me the significance of the last name she'd used or the one she eventually confessed to. And now I'd realized that her new last name—Parker—matched that of one of my biggest rivals, and he'd actually called me to ask whether I was still working with her, and my suspicions were growing by leaps and bounds.

I hated that I suspected her. But I'd been in business long enough to know that when my instincts told me that something seemed off, I needed to listen to those instincts rather than writing them off.

I didn't believe in coincidences. Mark Parker coming to me and trying to force me to sell to him, and a girl who happened to share his name showing up at my front door—or at least the side pathway that led to that door—and then getting into the company and dealing with the money itself...

Yes, I'd already been through all the ways that things weren't that simple. She hadn't wanted anything to do with me. She hadn't wanted to take the contract I offered her, and she hadn't wanted to work in my office. She'd basically been fighting me about working for me from the moment she started, and when she saw a way out, she'd taken it as quickly as she could. She'd also used that as an excuse to start trying to extricate herself from my life entirely.

But wouldn't a really talented spy have done all of that on purpose? Wouldn't she have made it look like she didn't want anything to do with me, just to throw me off and make sure I didn't get suspicious when I found out the in-between details? It seemed to me that things like that would have been taught in Corporate Spying 101.

Still, if she was who I was starting to suspect she was, why had she told me her real last name? Why hadn't she just maintained the idea that she was Olivia Cadwell to keep me off the case?

Yeah, Pete had discovered that she might not have come from Sunnyvale, but couldn't she just have easily said she lied about where she was from? it would have kept her from having to tell me a name that was the same as Mark Parker's.

But what was she to him? That was my next question, and I didn't have anything that even looked like a possible answer. I'd thought she might be his daughter, at first, but that didn't seem to make sense. She'd said her dad left before she was born, so why would she have his last name? How would she even know him?

Had he really left before she was born, though? What if that was just another lie?

I threw my head back against the back of my chair, groaning. So many questions. No answers. And each question was just making me more frustrated because it led to other questions. At this point I didn't even know if I believed that her real name was Olivia.

And I hated that. Because I really, really liked the girl.

I liked her enough that I knew I was going to end up giving her a chance to explain herself before I believed any of the insane speculations I'd just been through. I wanted to hear her story. I wanted to hear her version of things.

I wanted her to convince me that I was insane to suspect her. And then I wanted her to say that she'd stay with me rather than leaving.

Yeah, I saw the contradictions there. And I didn't give one single damn.

. . ∽ . .

I GOT HOME THINKING I knew exactly what I was going to say to her. I wanted to present my case but do it in a way that opened the door for her to talk to me rather than shutting down or feeling defensive. I wanted to make sure she knew that I had questions... but also that I was completely willing to believe pretty much anything she said to me.

Basically, if she was going to tell me what was going on, I was going to believe her. I wanted to believe her. I wanted her to have a completely innocent explanation, and I wanted it to be good enough that it took care of any questions I had in the future.

It wasn't good business to have that attitude. It was a really, really dangerous way to run a company, not only because I wasn't looking out for the company's best interests but because I was actively putting my personal feelings—and the word of a girl I barely knew—over and above those best interests.

If anyone else had been doing it, I would have fired them.

I still walked into my apartment knowing that it was exactly what I was going to do. I needed to get her side of the story, and I was going to give her a chance to give it to me herself rather than jumping the gun. I'd actually canceled a meeting with Pete, the PI, specifically to give Olivia a chance first.

When I walked through to the kitchen, though, coming up with the script I was going to use to start the conversation, I emerged to something I hadn't been even remotely expecting.

The entire place was covered in clutter, all of the countertops holding serving dishes, bowls, mixers, paper towels, and a range of ingredients too diverse to really take in. My eyes flew from object to object, trying to figure out what I was looking at, and finally came to rest on Olivia.

Or at least her back.

She was dressed a whole lot more casually than the last time I'd seen her, yesterday in the board meeting. Jeans and a tank top, both black, with her hair up in a messy bun on top of her head.

She was also covered in flour, from head to foot.

When she whirled around, shrieked, and started running toward me, I saw that it was also all over her face, though it was smeared with what I really hoped was chocolate sauce as well.

She threw herself into my arms before I could fully prepare, and the two of us went to the floor, flour dust exploding around us when we hit and making us both cough.

"Oh shit, are you okay?" she asked, shoving up off of me and looking at me with horrified eyes.

I coughed and sat up, afraid to look at what she'd done to my suit. "I'm fine," I said hoarsely. "Next time you're planning to leap on me, though, some warning might be nice."

She made a face, abashed. "I'm sorry. I just got so excited to see you. I guess I lost control."

She stood and gave me a hand up, and I went back to looking around the kitchen.

"Why does it look like a bomb went off in my pantry?" I asked. Then I glanced at her. "And why does it look like you were the bomb?"

She gave me an only sort of embarrassed grin. "What, the flour? You don't think it goes well with the outfit?"

"How did you manage to get it..." I made a circling motion with my hand, indicating her entire body. "Everywhere? Have you never... Have you never worked with flour before?"

Now she made a completely sarcastic face at me. "I've worked with it a lot, actually. But as for this... Well, I dropped a full bag. And it was open at the time. It turns out that when you drop a bag of flour at your feet, it sort of... explodes all over you."

I started laughing at the mental image of that, and the laughter felt so good after what I'd been thinking about all day that I quickly found that I didn't want to stop. Before long, Olivia was joining me, wiping at her face and getting more chocolate sauce on her forehead, then looking at me like I'd somehow caused the mess.

I howled at that one, and by the time I'd fond the paper towels and helped her to clean her face off, at least, I had tears streaming down my face and my cheeks were hurting.

"What, exactly, are you doing?" I asked. A deep breath told me that there was food in the oven, cooking, and another quick glance at the countertops showed a range of cookies and cakes there, half of them iced.

"Cooking," she told me blandly.

"Looks more like baking."

She grabbed my arm and shoved me right toward the goodies that looked finished. "You're right, actually. Baking. Because I've been thinking about what we were talking about. The bakery, you know?

Only I've made it a café. And a coffee shop. And a place that sells other drinks, too, because coffee doesn't go with every meal that I'm planning. And I had this thought about the menu and what I could do and..."

And with that, she was off, taking turns between shoving food at me and telling me to try it and explaining what it was and what she wanted to do with it. If she'd made a recipe up from scratch, she told me so and told me how she'd altered what someone else had done. And in between talking about the dishes she was serving me, she talked about the bakery itself.

Olivia's, she said with pride. She was going to call it Olivia's. And it was going to be a combination bakery/café/coffee shop/bookstore someday, and they were going to have the most amazing menu ever, and the menu was going to be some sort of revolving thing, though I didn't understand how exactly that would work.

When I said as much, she launched off into how it would work and how brilliant it was and how it would draw customers, and within a couple of moments, I was just as excited as she was about the whole idea.

The revolving menu thing was... brilliant. It was really, really smart. A whole lot smarter than anything I'd ever imagined when it came to a restaurant. I'd heard a lot of pitches for eateries, and I'd never been that impressed with them.

Partially, I thought, because they weren't presented by a woman that I wanted to drag right to bed with me. But partially because the ideas she was presenting were really, really good.

And never mind the food she was feeding me. Yes, it was all sweets, and I hadn't had anything to eat for lunch and could really have used something more substantial, but I had flavors exploding in my mouth that I'd never dreamed of, and though I'd thought she was crazy to talk about combing chili peppers and chocolate in the same cake, I was now sailing through my second slice and wondering if I could place a weekly order for it.

"Olivia," I told her, my mouth full. "This is freaking delicious."

"I know!" she exploded. "And I totally made that recipe up, can you believe it? I just thought, what if I try this and that together and see how it goes? And it turns out it's genius!"

I looked at her with renewed wonder. "I honestly didn't even know you could cook."

She shrugged. "That's because you're always so busy taking over in the kitchen. You never gave me a chance."

She was right. I'd never even asked whether she could cook. I'd just taken over.

Sort of like I still hadn't bothered to ask her about her relationship to Mark Parker. Which was what I was supposed to be doing right now.

I slid past that thought and asked to try one of the cookies I hadn't tried yet. The discussion about Mark Parker could wait.

Right now, I just wanted to enjoy listening to her get more excited than I'd ever heard her. I wanted to hear more about this idea of hers.

I wanted to see whether I could help her make it happen.

CHAPTER 25

OLIVIA

I WOKE UP THE NEXT morning just as excited as I had been when I went to bed, and my brain immediately started whirring through my plans for Olivia's.

Leo had been in love with everything I cooked, and we'd spent the hour after he got home cleaning up the kitchen and brainstorming additional business ideas. He'd had a lot of really good feedback in terms of the business side of things and had even recommended a couple of people he knew who owned buildings that had restaurant space in them. I'd wished more than once that I'd been taking notes rather than cleaning flour out of every nook and cranny in the kitchen, but I'd also told myself that he was so smart that he'd be able to remember everything he said and probably repeat it verbatim if I needed him to.

Besides, I was still going to be here for two more days. That was plenty of time to ask him to repeat anything that I hadn't gotten down.

I jumped out of bed and ran for the shower, going through the steps I wanted to take today. I had two more days here, which meant I had two days of freedom before I had to start thinking about finding a place to live and potentially another job. I knew that this was going to take most of my time, but I also knew it was going to cost a lot.

Yes, Leo had offered to invest in the place. I'd told him no. I'd saved the paychecks I made at his company and would have the money he paid me for having acted as his arm candy for a couple of weeks, and I thought it would get me started.

I also had the money Sonya had given me as my one and only investor. I hadn't told Leo about that part. I didn't want to have to tell him why I'd accepted money from her when I wouldn't accept it from him, and I certainly didn't want to tell him why I thought it would be easier to have her onboard than him.

Partially because I wasn't completely sure of the answer myself. I just knew that my gut was screaming at me not to take money from him and not to accept him as an investor in the café. Things were already so complicated between us, and getting money involved—or the risk of a new endeavor like this—seemed like it would make things even worse.

Maybe I'd let him invest once I had a better idea of how well it would work. Once I knew he wouldn't be disappointed. But I wasn't even really sure about that.

I turned on the shower and closed the door, knowing now that it would take only about thirty seconds to get to the temperature I wanted. When Leo had promised me plenty of hot water, he definitely hadn't been lying.

It was one of the things I'd be missing the most when I left here.

I turned to face myself in the mirror and started stripping, my eyes meeting my own gaze and staring back at me.

When I left.

Two days.

Shit, I wasn't ready.

And at the same time, I thought that the sooner I left, and the sooner I eliminated any danger Roger might bring Leo's way, the better.

. . ⚜ . .

"DO YOU REALLY THINK it's a good idea to do that many different kinds of cookies, though?" Alice asked.

I put the phone on my shoulder and held it against my ear, needing my hands for mixing and then rolling a new recipe of peanut butter oatmeal cookies I was trying out. "I mean, our first label is 'bakery,' so I don't feel like we can ever actually have too many baked goods," I said firmly. "It's sort of in the name, you know? But I figure that will also be a big part of the revolving menu, at least at first. Or maybe I'll do a different revolving menu that has a new secret cookie every month. And we'll do a deal where you can get an entire dozen secret menu cookies at a discount!"

The new idea exploded through my brain like fireworks, ideas sprouting up everywhere the sparks landed and moving so quickly that I almost couldn't grab them before they were replaced by new ideas.

"Or we can have themes! Secret Menu Chocolate Chip vs. Secret Menu Oatmeal vs Secret Menu Sugar Cookies! Brilliant!"

Alice giggled. "Your secret menu is going to be more interesting than your regular menu!"

"That's sort of the idea. It's like a secret club, you know? Once you know about it, you're on the inside and you can get all this stuff no one else even knows about!"

"I don't think I've ever heard you so excited about anything," she replied, her voice still filled with laughter. "Not even that award you won when we were kids for reading more books than anyone else in our grade."

"That was a great reward," I said, remembering the little trophy I'd won. "But it didn't come with thirteen flavors of cookies. Or a café literally named after me. How are you doing on the packing?"

Alice had agreed to come out and be my first employee, and I couldn't wait to see my best friend again. Though I'd made her promise to leave Sunnyvale in the middle of the night and pull over every half an hour to make sure no one was tailing her.

I just didn't trust Roger not to be watching her. Of all the people in that town, he had to know that I was most likely to reach out to Alice—and she was the one most likely to come to me if the opportunity presented itself. I still didn't entirely understand what he wanted from me, though my mom's idea that he thought I'd stolen money from him was definitely a start, but I wouldn't put it past him to try to use Alice to get to me.

I also wouldn't be surprised if he actually tried to hurt her just to show me what was waiting for me if I didn't do whatever it was he wanted me to do.

But that was not something to think about right now.

"You have plenty of gas in your car?" I asked.

"Even if I didn't, I'm going to be pulling over often enough that I could make sure one of those stops was at a gas station."

"Okay, that's true. But I don't like the idea of you being out of the car in the middle of the night."

"And yet it's okay for me to be driving through mostly deserted land in the middle of the night?"

"Driving in the dark is different from being out and about at a gas station in the dark," I said sharply. "I might want you to pull over to see if anyone is behind you. I don't want you getting out of the car at all, understand?"

I heard the face she was making at me. And I'd known Alice long enough to know exactly what it looked like.

"I can see you making a face at me," I muttered.

"Good. Then you'll know what I'm going to say next, which is that you're worrying too much and that I've driven by myself before and know how to do it," she returned quickly. "Olivia. I'll be fine. Stop worrying about me and start worrying about yourself. Do you know where you're going to be staying when you leave Leo's?"

My heart, which had been floating somewhere five feet above me at the thought that I was going to start Olivia's soon and do it with Alice at my side, dropped quite suddenly to the floor.

Leave Leo's. I still hated that it was going to come down to that. I knew it was the right thing, and I knew that it was what I had to do. I had too much baggage riding along on my back to be safe for Leo himself, and I wasn't going to put him in danger.

I cared way too much about him.

But I hated that it was the right answer, and I hated that it meant I had to leave him. I'd never meant to find him, and I'd fought it tooth and nail at first. I'd walked away from him more than once and thought he was joking when he first told me that he wanted to pay me to hang out with him.

Hell, I'd been trying to quit for days before he finally accepted it and let me go. I'd been talking myself out of falling in love with him basically since the moment I walked into his house.

But somewhere in between him catching me in the phone booth the first time and right now, when I was actively planning my exit from his apartment, in the midst of long nights talking in bed and an insane night of playing Nintendo, I'd gone ahead and fallen in love with him.

I'd known it for a couple of days now, but hadn't been admitting it to myself.

Mostly because it didn't change anything. I still had to leave, and knowing that I was in love with him would just make leaving even harder.

"I have a hotel already lined up," I said, remembering that I was supposed to be answering Alice's question rather than having a mental argument with myself. "I'll be there for the first week, and that gives me some time to shop for an apartment. Don't worry; I got a room that has a bed for you, too."

"And have you told Leo that you're still going to be in town? Or are you expecting him to somehow not notice?"

I bit my lip. "The second option. We'll be across town, in the non-business district. Minneapolis is an awfully big city, Alice. With luck, he'll never even realize that a new bakery/café/coffee shop has opened downtown."

I was counting on it.

Because once I walked out of this apartment and said goodbye to him, I didn't want to see him again. Seeing him again would just make me want to come running back to his hot water, cooking, and the sexy, gorgeous looks he gave me when we woke up in the same bed.

· · ❧ · ·

WHEN LEO GOT HOME, he walked into the apartment like something was very, very wrong. And where he'd laughed at the mess I'd made in the kitchen yesterday, today he looked at it like I had somehow betrayed him by cooking without him.

My heart cracked a little bit at the look. I didn't know what I'd done to disappoint him so much or what it had to do with the mess I'd made in the kitchen, but my emotions, which had been flying high all day with thoughts about recipes and Olivia's and the space I had an appointment to look at tomorrow, suddenly felt like they'd become rain clouds.

Big black ones. The kind that came with wind and lightning and thunder and cold temperatures.

I'd been on an excited high all day. Now I suddenly felt like everything had come crashing back to earth. And I didn't like it.

"What's wrong?" I asked, already afraid of what he was going to say.

Please just say you had a bad day. Please just say you had a bad day, I chanted in my head. If it was nothing more than a bad day, then it wasn't my fault. It had nothing to do with me. It didn't mean he'd decided that he didn't actually like me at all and was going to kick me out right now rather than giving me another day.

He just shrugged and sat stiffly in the barstool nearest to him, his face still serious and his eyes on mine.

"What's going on with you?" I asked.

"Nothing. Why?"

"Because you don't usually sit there and stare at me like you're about to tell me that my best friend turned out to be a zombie and started the zombie apocalypse, and we now have to get the hell out of here before they show up at our door. Mainly. Are we expecting zombies momentarily?"

The corner of his mouth twitched like some part of him wanted to smile at the joke, but it didn't make it all the way to a smile, and it definitely didn't make it all the way to his eyes. Those, their blue dark and cloudy now, stayed completely serious.

Right, so evidently it wasn't a time for jokes.

"So... no zombies?" I asked weakly.

I'd never known Leo to refuse a joke before. I mean no, I hadn't known him that long, but I'd been around him an awful lot over the last two weeks, and I was starting to think I knew him at least a little bit. More than I knew a lot of people.

More than I knew most people because I'd never been someone who kept a lot of friends around. I just wasn't good at dealing with people. Never had been. And that didn't really bother me. I kept myself happy with the few people I felt really got me.

And up until right now, I'd sort of thought Leo was one of those people.

Not that I was planning to stay with him. I couldn't afford to do that. But thinking that he might not understand me—or might not want to—broke something inside of me that I hadn't realized was even there.

"Leo?" I whispered. "What's going on? You're acting... weird."

He closed his eyes as if he was trying to decide on something and pinched his nose, which I knew from experience meant he was definitely trying to puzzle something out in his mind.

He'd done the same thing when he was trying to figure out what to do about the board, and shit, was there something going on with the company that I didn't know about yet? Had I already fallen behind on the company news? Or was it the new girl already messing things up?

Did he need me to go back in and fix something? Because I would, I realized. I didn't want to work there, but if something was wrong and I could fix it, I would do it in a heartbeat.

I was just about to say so when he finally started talking.

"I saw you talking to Mark Parker outside of my office that day, and I watched you flush and then get away from him as quickly as you could. And then I watched him watch you walk away, looking like he'd just seen a ghost," he said quietly. "And then when I asked you about it, you said you didn't know him. But I was right above you. I saw how you looked at him and how he looked at you, and I knew that there was more to it than that."

Oh crap. Mark Parker. Yes, I knew him. I'd never met him personally, but I'd seen pictures of him. Old pictures, but he hadn't changed much.

Yes, I'd recognized him immediately. And he must have seen pictures of me, too, because he'd recognized me, as well.

I just hadn't known that Leo had been able to see all that. So when he'd asked me about Mark, I'd lied and said I didn't know him. At the time, I'd thought that was the better, easier option.

Now I was starting to think I'd been wrong.

"I was curious, and I knew you weren't going to tell me anything," he continued, "and since Mark was there to try to buy my company, again, I decide that this was a matter of company business. This wasn't just personal curiosity. So I called my PI and asked him to ask around and find out how you two were connected."

All the nice thoughts I'd been having about him flew right out the window.

"You what?" I gasped. "You called the PI and set him on me again? I thought you said you wouldn't do that! Leo, I thought you said you'd come to me with questions if you had them in the future!"

And I almost walked out right then and there, too betrayed and horrified to stay in his presence any longer. I'd liked this man. I'd thought I was in love with him. And yet there he was, making promises he'd immediately broken and snooping into my life—again—despite the fact that there was nothing to find!

He reached out and grabbed my arm, though, stopping me from moving away.

"Why didn't you tell me you were married?"

That stopped me better than his grip would have done.

"What?" I gasped again. "Married? Leo, what the hell are you talking about?"

I'd never been married. I'd never even considered it.

He got a phone call before he could answer, and I watched him answer it, not even surprised anymore that he'd take a phone call in the middle of a conversation like this.

He seemed inclined to take phone calls at the worst possible time. Or maybe he was just trying to delay the inevitable. Because my mind was already packing the remains of my clothes and handing me dramatic lines to use as I stormed out of the apartment, too betrayed by this man to stay one second longer.

When he got off the phone, though, he looked... shocked. Disappointed.

He looked like a man who was very, very sorry to have been right.

"He's your dad."

It wasn't a question. It was a statement. And I realized that I had two choices right now: I could either tell him the truth and finally come clean... or I could deny it and get the hell out of there, never to see Leo Folley again.

The question was... which one was I going to pick?

THE END

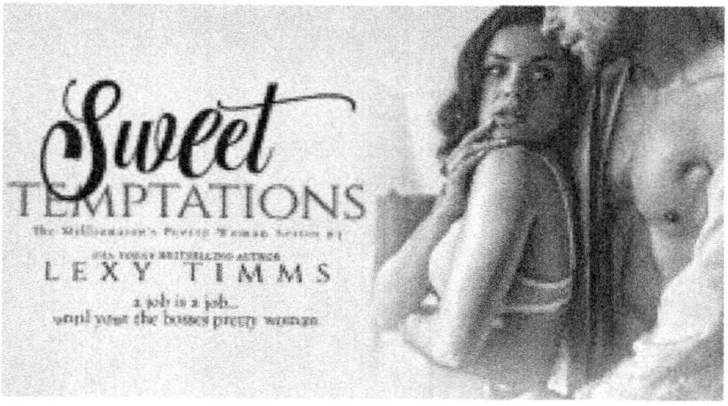
Sweet
TEMPTATIONS
LEXY TIMMS
a job is a job...

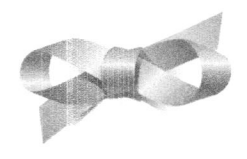

The Millionaire's Pretty Woman Series

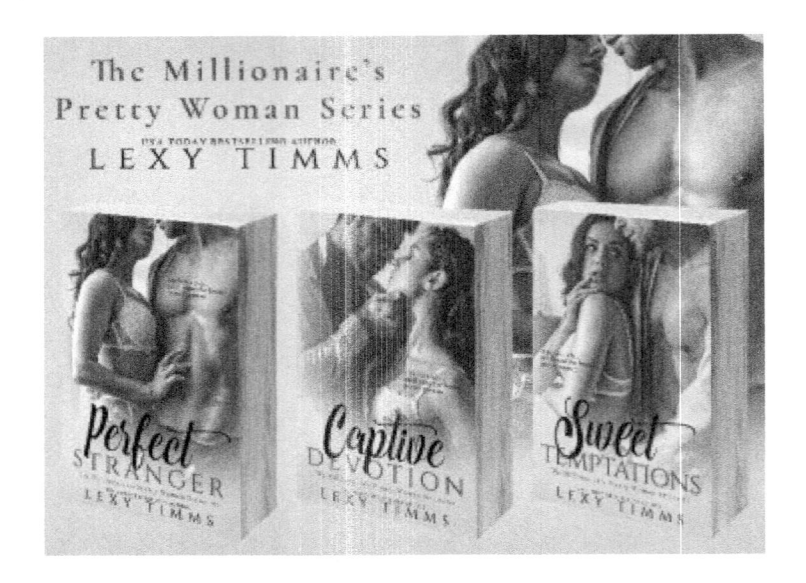

Book 1 – Perfect Stranger
Book 2 – Captive Devotion
Book 3 – Sweet Temptations

Strength & Style Series

NOW AVAILABLE!!
Book 1 – Suits You, Sir
Book 2 – Tailor Made
Book 3 – Perfect Gentleman

Find Lexy Timms:

LEXY TIMMS NEWSLETTER:
http://eepurl.com/9i0vD
Lexy Timms Facebook Page:
https://www.facebook.com/SavingForever
Lexy Timms Website:
http://www.lexytimms.com

Want

FREE READS?

Sign up for Lexy Timms' newsletter
And she'll send you updates on new releases,
ARC copies of books and a whole lotta fun!

Sign up for news and updates!
http://eepurl.com/9i0vD

More by Lexy Timms:

FROM BEST SELLING AUTHOR, Lexy Timms, comes a billionaire romance that'll make you swoon and fall in love all over again.

Jamie Connors has given up on men. Despite being smart, pretty, and just slightly overweight, she's a magnet for the kind of guys that don't stay around.

Her sister's wedding is at the foreground of the family's attention. Jamie would be fine with it if her sister wasn't pressuring her to lose weight so she'll fit in the maid of honor dress, her mother would get off her case and her ex-boyfriend wasn't about to become her brother-in-law.

Determined to step out on her own, she accepts a PA position from billionaire Alex Reid. The job includes an apartment on his property and gets her out of living in her parent's basement.

Jamie must balance her life and somehow figure out how to manage her billionaire boss, without falling in love with him.

** The Boss is book 1 in the Managing the Bosses series. All your questions won't be answered in the first book. It may end on a cliff hanger.

For mature audiences only. There are adult situations, but this is a love story, NOT erotica.

Book 1 – Payment for Sin
Book 2 – Atonement Within
Book 3 – Declaration of Love

Faking It Description:

HE GROANED. THIS WAS torture. Being trapped in a room with a beautiful woman was just about every man's fantasy, but he had to remember that this was just pretend.

Allyson Smith has crushed on her boss for years, but never dared to make a move. When she finds herself without a date to her brother's upcoming wedding, Allyson tells her family one innocent white lie: that she's been dating her boss. Unfortunately, her boss discovers her lie, and insists on posing as her boyfriend to escort her to the wedding.

Playboy billionaire Dane Prescott always has a new heiress on his arm, but he can't get his assistant Allyson out of his head. He's fought his attraction to her, until he gets caught up in her scheme of a fake relationship.

One passionate weekend with the boss has Allyson Smith questioning everything she believes in. Falling for a wealthy playboy like Dane is against the rules, but if she's just faking it what's the harm?

SOMETIMES THE HEART needs a different kind of saving... find out if Charity Thompson will find a way of saving forever in this hospital setting Best-Selling Romance by Lexy Timms

CAPTIVE DEVOTION

Charity Thompson wants to save the world, one hospital at a time. Instead of finishing med school to become a doctor, she chooses a different path and raises money for hospitals – new wings, equipment, whatever they need. Except there is one hospital she would be happy to never set foot in again—her fathers. So of course, he hires her to create a gala for his sixty-fifth birthday. Charity can't say no. Now she is working in the one place she doesn't want to be. Except she's attracted to Dr. Elijah Bennet, the handsome playboy chief.

Will she ever prove to her father that's she's more than a med school dropout? Or will her attraction to Elijah keep her from repairing the one thing she desperately wants to fix?

THE ONE YOU CAN'T FORGET

Emily Rose Dougherty is a good Catholic girl from mythical Walkerville, CT. She had somehow managed to get herself into a heap trouble with the law, all because an ex-boyfriend has decided to make things difficult.

Luke "Spade" Wade owns a Motorcycle repair shop and is the Road Captain for Hades' Spawn MC. He's shocked when he reads in the paper that his old high school flame has been arrested. She's always been the one he couldn't forget.

Will destiny let them find each other again? Or what happens in the past, best left for the history books?

** *This is book 1 of the Hades' Spawn MC Series. All your questions may not be answered in the first book.*

Download For
FREE
Lexy
Timmins
BILLIONAIRE BIKER
LEXY TIMMS

• • ❧ • •

THE
DEAD OF NIGHT
SERIES
LEXY TIMMS
Abduction
Bribery
Corruption

THE
HEAT OF NIGHT
SERIES
USA TODAY BESTSELLING AUTHOR
LEXY TIMMS
Depravity
Scandal
Disgrace

Don't miss out!

Visit the website below and you can sign up to receive emails whenever Lexy Timms publishes a new book. There's no charge and no obligation.

https://books2read.com/r/B-A-NNL-COLQB

BOOKS 2 READ

Connecting independent readers to independent writers.

Did you love *Captive Devotion*? Then you should read *Devil's Bay*[1] by Lexy Timms!

USA Today Bestselling Author, Lexy Timms, weaves a story of loss, danger, and risking it all for love.

Always have an escape plan...

Claire Carpenter is haunted by tragedy. When her brother is found murdered, she swears to get justice and find his killer. However, the police in small-town Devil's Bay are running out of leads and ready to drop the case. The chance for justice dwindles until the handsome FBI agent sent to investigate arrives and reawakens a desire Claire buried a long time ago.

As a seasoned field agent, Fletcher Hughes knows how to track killers. But Claire Carpenter is more than the FBI agent bargained for.

---

1. https://books2read.com/u/boDJXp

2. https://books2read.com/u/boDJXp

With the opportunity to kill, Claire instantly becomes his lead suspect in the case and Fletcher is ready to harden his already frozen heart. Too bad gorgeous Claire stirs his blood and makes him want to rewrite the rules.

When more bodies start to pile up Fletcher is determined to stick to Claire and see the case through, because it doesn't matter if the killer on the loose is Claire Carpenter herself or someone else in the shadows. He won't rest until he gets the truth. Even if he has to seduce her.

Betrayal At The Bay Series:
Devil's Bay
Devil's Deceit
Devil's Duplicity
Read more at www.lexytimms.com.

Also by Lexy Timms

A Bad Boy Bullied Romance
I Hate You
I Hate You A Little Bit
I Hate You A Little Bit More

A Bump in the Road Series
Expecting Love
Selfless Act
Doctor's Orders

A Burning Love Series
Spark of Passion
Flame of Desire
Blaze of Ecstasy

A Chance at Forever Series
Forever Perfect
Forever Desired

Forever Together

A Dark Mafia Romance Series
Taken By The Mob Boss
Truce With The Mob Boss
Taking Over the Mob Boss
Trouble For The Mob Boss
Tailored By The Mob Boss
Tricking the Mob Boss

A Dating App Series
I've Been Matched
You've Been Matched
We've Been Matched

A "Kind of" Billionaire
Taking a Risk
Safety in Numbers
Pretend You're Mine

A Maybe Series
Maybe I Should
Maybe I Shouldn't
Maybe I Did

Assisting the Boss Series
Billion Reasons
Duke of Delegation
Late Night Meetings
Delegating Love
Suitors and Admirers

BBW Romance Series
Capturing Her Beauty
Pursuing Her Dreams
Tracing Her Curves

Beating the Biker Series
Making Her His
Making the Break
Making of Them

Betrayal at the Bay Series
Devil's Bay
Devil's Deceit
Devil's Duplicity

Billionaire Banker Series
Banking on Him

Price of Passion
Investing in Love
Knowing Your Worth
Treasured Forever
Banking on Christmas
Billionaire Banker Box Set Books #1-3

Billionaire CEO Brothers
Tempting the Player
Late Night Boardroom
Reviewing the Perfomance
Result of Passion
Directing the Next Move
Touching the Assets

Billionaire Hitman Series
The Hit
The Job
The Run

Billionaire Holiday Romance Series
Driving Home for Christmas
The Valentine Getaway
Cruising Love
Billionaire Holiday Romance Box Set

Billionaire in Disguise Series
Facade
Illusion
Charade

Billionaire Secrets Series
The Secret
Freedom
Courage
Trust
Impulse
Billionaire Secrets Box Set Books #1-3

Blind Sight Series
See Me
Fix Me
Eyes On Me

Branded Series
Money or Nothing
What People Say
Give and Take

Building Billions

Building Billions - Part 1
Building Billions - Part 2
Building Billions - Part 3

Butler & Heiress Series
To Serve
For Duty
No Chore
All Wrapped Up

Change of Heart Series
The Heart Needs
The Heart Wants
The Heart Knows

Counting the Billions
Counting the Days
Counting On You
Counting the Kisses

Cry Wolf Reverse Harem Series
Beautiful & Wild
Misunderstood
Never Tamed

Darkest Night Series
Savage
Vicious
Brutal
Sinful
Fierce

Diamond in the Rough Anthology
Billionaire Rock
Billionaire Rock - part 2

Dirty Little Taboo Series
Flirting Touch
Denying Pleasure
Forbidding Desire
Craving Passion

Dominating PA Series
Her Personal Assistant - Part 1
Her Personal Assistant - Part 2
Her Personal Assistant Box Set

Fake Billionaire Series
Faking It

Temporary CEO
Caught in the Act
Never Tell A Lie
Fake Christmas
Fake Billionaire Box Set #1-3

Firehouse Romance Series
Caught in Flames
Burning With Desire
Craving the Heat
Firehouse Romance Complete Collection

Forging Billions Series
Dirty Money
Petty Cash
Payment Required

For His Pleasure
Elizabeth
Georgia
Madison

Fortune Riders MC Series
Billionaire Biker
Billionaire Ransom
Billionaire Misery

Fortune Riders Box Set - Books #1-3

Fragile Series
Fragile Touch
Fragile Kiss
Fragile Love

Great Temptation Series
The Devil's Footsteps
Heaven's Command
Mortals Surrender

Hades' Spawn Motorcycle Club
One You Can't Forget
One That Got Away
One That Came Back
One You Never Leave
One Christmas Night
Hades' Spawn MC Complete Series

Hard Rocked Series
Rhyme
Harmony
Lyrics

Heart of Stone Series
The Protector
The Guardian
The Warrior

Heart of the Battle Series
Celtic Viking
Celtic Rune
Celtic Mann
Heart of the Battle Series Box Set

Heistdom Series
Master Thief
Goldmine
Diamond Heist
Smile For Me
Your Move
Green With Envy
Saving Money

Highlander Wolf Series
Pack Run
Pack Land
Pack Rules

Hollyweird Fae Series
Inception of Gold
Disruption of Magic
Guardians of Twilight

How To Love A Spy
The Secret
The Secret Life
The Secret Wife

Just About Series
About Love
About Truth
About Forever
Just About Box Set Books #1-3

Justice Series
Seeking Justice
Finding Justice
Chasing Justice
Pursuing Justice
Justice - Complete Series

Karma Series

Walk Away
Make Him Pay
Perfect Revenge

Kissed by Billions
Kissed by Passion
Kissed by Desire
Kissed by Love

Leaning Towards Trouble
Trouble
Discord
Tenacity

Love on the Sea Series
Ships Ahoy
Rough Sea
High Tide

Love You Series
Love Life
Need Love
My Love

Managing the Billionaire

Never Enough
Worth the Cost
Secret Admirers
Chasing Affection
Pressing Romance
Timeless Memories
Managing the Billionaire Box Set Books #1-3

Managing the Bosses Series
The Boss
The Boss Too
Who's the Boss Now
Love the Boss
I Do the Boss
Wife to the Boss
Employed by the Boss
Brother to the Boss
Senior Advisor to the Boss
Forever the Boss
Christmas With the Boss
Billionaire in Control
Billionaire Makes Millions
Billionaire at Work
Precious Little Thing
Priceless Love
Valentine Love
The Cost of Freedom
Trick or Treat
The Night Before Christmas
Gift for the Boss - Novella 3.5
Managing the Bosses Box Set #1-3

Managing the Bosses Novellas

Mislead by the Bad Boy Series
Deceived
Provoked
Betrayed

Model Mayhem Series
Shameless
Modesty
Imperfection

Moment in Time
Highlander's Bride
Victorian Bride
Modern Day Bride
A Royal Bride
Forever the Bride

Mountain Millionaire Series
Close to the Ridge
Crossing the Bluff
Climbing the Mount

My Best Friend's Sister

Hometown Calling
A Perfect Moment
Thrown in Together

My Darker Side Series
Darkest Hour
Time to Stop
Against the Light

Neverending Dream Series
Neverending Dream - Part 1
Neverending Dream - Part 2
Neverending Dream - Part 3
Neverending Dream - Part 4
Neverending Dream - Part 5
Neverending Dream Box Set Books #1-3

Outside the Octagon
Submit
Fight
Knockout

Protecting Diana Series
Her Bodyguard
Her Defender
Her Champion

Her Protector
Her Forever
Protecting Diana Box Set Books #1-3

Protecting Layla Series
His Mission
His Objective
His Devotion

Racing Hearts Series
Rush
Pace
Fast

Regency Romance Series
The Duchess Scandal - Part 1
The Duchess Scandal - Part 2

Reverse Harem Series
Primals
Archaic
Unitary

R&S Rich and Single Series
Alex Reid

Parker
Sebastian

Saving Forever
Saving Forever - Part 1
Saving Forever - Part 2
Saving Forever - Part 3
Saving Forever - Part 4
Saving Forever - Part 5
Saving Forever - Part 6
Saving Forever Part 7
Saving Forever - Part 8
Saving Forever Boxset Books #1-3

Secrets & Lies Series
Strange Secrets
Evading Secrets
Inspiring Secrets
Lies and Secrets
Mastering Secrets
Alluring Secrets
Secrets & Lies Box Set Books #1-3

Shifting Desires Series
Jungle Heat
Jungle Fever
Jungle Blaze

Sin Series
Payment for Sin
Atonement Within
Declaration of Love

Southern Romance Series
Little Love Affair
Siege of the Heart
Freedom Forever
Soldier's Fortune

Spanked Series
Passion
Playmate
Pleasure

Spelling Love Series
The Author
The Book Boyfriend
The Words of Love

Strength & Style
Suits You, Sir
Tailor Made

Taboo Wedding Series
He Loves Me Not
With This Ring
Happily Ever After

Tattooist Series
Confession of a Tattooist
Surrender of a Tattooist
Heart of a Tattooist
Hopes & Dreams of a Tattooist

Tennessee Romance
Whisky Lullaby
Whisky Melody
Whisky Harmony

The Bad Boy Alpha Club
Battle Lines - Part 1
Battle Lines

The Brush Of Love Series
Every Night
Every Day
Every Time

Every Way
Every Touch
The Brush of Love Series Box Set Books #1-3

The City of Mayhem Series
True Mayhem
Relentless Chaos

The Debt
The Debt: Part 1 - Damn Horse
The Debt: Complete Collection

The Fire Inside Series
Dare Me
Defy Me
Burn Me

The Gentleman's Club Series
Gambler
Player
Wager

The Golden Mail
Hot Off the Press
Extra! Extra!

Read All About It
Stop the Press
Breaking News
This Just In
The Golden Mail Box Set Books #1-3

The Lucky Billionaire Series
Lucky Break
Streak of Luck
Lucky in Love

The Millionaire's Pretty Woman Series
Perfect Stranger
Captive Devotion
Sweet Temptations

The Sound of Breaking Hearts Series
Disruption
Destroy
Devoted

The University of Gatica Series
The Recruiting Trip
Faster
Higher
Stronger

Dominate
No Rush
University of Gatica - The Complete Series

T.N.T. Series
Troubled Nate Thomas - Part 1
Troubled Nate Thomas - Part 2
Troubled Nate Thomas - Part 3

Toxic Touch Series
Noxious
Lethal
Willful
Tainted
Craved
Toxic Touch Box Set Books #1-3

Undercover Boss Series
Marketing
Finance
Legal

Undercover Series
Perfect For Me
Perfect For You
Perfect For Us

Unknown Identity Series
Unknown
Unpublished
Unexposed
Unsure
Unwritten
Unknown Identity Box Set: Books #1-3

Unlucky Series
Unlucky in Love
UnWanted
UnLoved Forever

War Torn Letters Series
My Sweetheart
My Darling
My Beloved

Wet & Wild Series
Stormy Love
Savage Love
Secure Love

Worth It Series

Worth Billions
Worth Every Cent
Worth More Than Money

You & Me - A Bad Boy Romance
Just Me
Touch Me
Kiss Me

Standalone
Wash
Loving Charity
Summer Lovin'
Love & College
Billionaire Heart
First Love
Frisky and Fun Romance Box Collection
Beating Hades' Bikers
Everyone Loves a Bad Boy

Watch for more at www.lexytimms.com.

About the Author

"Love should be something that lasts forever, not is lost forever." Visit USA TODAY BESTSELLING AUTHOR, LEXY TIMMS https://www.facebook.com/SavingForever *Please feel free to connect with me and share your comments. I love connecting with my readers.* Sign up for news and updates and freebies - I like spoiling my readers! http://eepurl.com/9i0vD website: www.lexytimms.com Dealing in Antique Jewelry and hanging out with her awesome hubby and three kids, Lexy Timms loves writing in her free time. MANAGING THE BOSSES is a bestselling 10-part series dipping into the lives of Alex Reid and Jamie Connors. Can a secretary really fall for her billionaire boss?

Read more at www.lexytimms.com.

Printed in Great Britain
by Amazon